BY MICHAEL BUCKLEY

The Sisters Grimm

Book One: The Fairy-Tale Detectives

Book Two: The Unusual Suspects

Book Three: The Problem Child

Book Four: Once Upon a Crime

Book Five: Magic and Other Misdemeanors

Book Six: Tales from the Hood

Book Seven: The Everafter War

Book Eight: The Inside Story

NERDS

Book One: National Espionage, Rescue, and Defense Society

Book Two: M Is for Mama's Boy

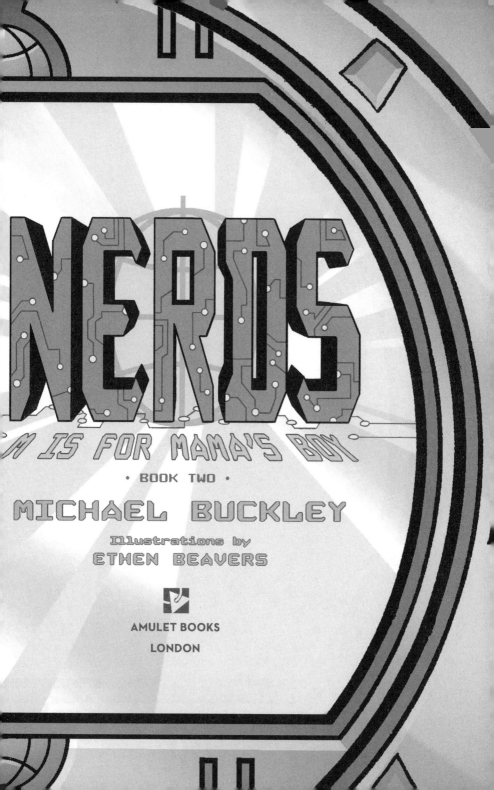

NERDS

M IS FOR MAMA'S BOY

· BOOK TWO ·

MICHAEL BUCKLEY

Illustrations by
ETHEN BEAVERS

AMULET BOOKS

LONDON

ISBN 978-0-8109-9674-8

Text copyright © 2010 Michael Buckley
Illustrations copyright © 2010 Ethen Beavers

Book design by Chad W. Beckerman

Printed and bound in U.S.A.
10 9 8 7 6 5 4 3 2 1

ABRAMS
THE ART OF BOOKS SINCE 1949

The Market Building
72-82 Rosebery Avenue
London, UK EC1R 4RW
www.abramsbooks.co.uk

For Nikki Mock,
Janet Vaughan,
and all the kids
at Hammond Hill
Elementary in North
Augusta, South
Carolina: the place
where NERDS
was born.

Prologue

The goon woke in a hospital with a bandage wrapped tightly around his ribs and an IV dripping sedatives into a vein in his arm. Though he could not remember how he had been injured or how long he had been unconscious, his first thought was to call the office and find someone to cover his shifts. He had a busy week of beating people to a bloody pulp, and his victims weren't going to punch themselves in the face. He couldn't leave his bosses in the lurch. He was evil, but he was professional.

Perhaps it was his dedication to his work that had built him such an impressive résumé: fifteen broken jaws, fifty-seven legs, a hundred arms, and more noses than he could count. He had knocked out thousands of teeth, pushed a few people off bridges, and once buried a guy in concrete up to his neck. He had been nominated for Goon of the Year nine times by OUCH (Organization of United Criminals and Henchman), and had won its highest honor, the Brass Knuckle, seven times. At the office, he showed up early and left late. He had his lunch on the job, frequently beating people as he ate his peanut-butter-and-jelly sandwiches. You didn't get on the FBI's Ten Most Wanted list by taking a sick day! He leaned over to the IV line that fed his body sedatives and yanked out the needle. He couldn't have predicted how much it would sting. The pain brought back a wave of memories.

The goon had been in the employ of an eleven-year-old evil mastermind who wore a black mask with a white skull painted on it. It had been a fiasco. "Simon," as he called himself, had made some rookie mistakes that had led to bigger problems. His first mistake was working with a mad scientist named Dr. Jigsaw—a kook with a doomsday device that was supposed to pull Earth's continents back together. Second, the kid had spent a fortune building a secret fortress at the North Pole for said kook. Naturally, some heroes came along and destroyed the place just before the overly complicated plan could be unleashed on the world, which was Simon's third-biggest blunder; he should have killed the heroes as soon as they arrived. Instead, he took them hostage. Even babies know that heroes have a tendency to escape just in time and ruin a villain's plan. Sure enough, the heroes destroyed Dr. Jigsaw's continental-shift machine. During this calamity, something fell on the goon. Then everything went black and he woke up in this hospital.

Now the goon's cell phone rang. Someone had set it on the table next to him, and as he reached for it, he realized he was missing a hand! In its place was a hook. The goon studied it for a moment, then the closest thing to a smile his mouth had ever produced appeared on his face. Most people would have been devastated to see a menacing metal hook where their hand should be. Not the goon. The hook was just the kind of thing that would win him his eighth Brass Knuckle award.

He reached over with his real hand and snatched up the phone. When he saw that the caller ID said SIMON, he answered it.

"Hello," the boy's voice said over a tremendous racket. It sounded as if he were trapped in a storm. "It's me. I see you survived the explosion."

"Not quite. I lost a hand. I had a doctor clean it up. They put a hook on my arm."

"Cool," Simon said.

The goon almost smiled again. It *was* cool, but he didn't like to brag. "It actually hurts a lot and I have to give up the piano," he said.

"Oh. Your sacrifice is noted and appreciated."

"I'm sorry about the plan, boss," the goon said. Through the wind he heard laughing. Then again, it might have been a

cry for help. He couldn't be sure. "Boss? Are you OK? It sounds like you are laughing."

There was a long pause followed by a number of grunts and groans, then Simon's voice returned. "Your concern is amusing, my friend, but completely unnecessary. You see, Jigsaw and his little machine were just part of a much bigger plan, one that is going exactly the way I want. Take care of yourself. I'll contact you when I need you again."

Then the phone went dead.

"Hello, it's good to see you awake," a doctor said from the doorway. He was tall, with gray hair and a kind face. "I wanted to talk to you about your hand. I know you must be very troubled to find the hook—it sort of looks like a prop from a pirate movie. Fortunately, it's just temporary. We're ordering a new one that looks and acts a lot like a real hand. It should be here in a week."

In response, the goon tossed his pillow into the air, then used his hook to slash it in two. Feathers flew around the room. "Actually, I think this will be just fine."

Simon's plan was *not* going exactly the way he wanted. He was trapped on a tiny ledge on the side of an enormous ice mountain at the top of the world—the North Pole, to be exact. The temperature was just above negative 35 degrees Fahrenheit and in all directions there was little more than drifting ice sheets and glaciers. Firm ground was nearly a mile above, and the deadly cold waters of the Arctic Ocean were far below. He had been stranded on the ledge for two days, freezing, starving, and desperate for water. No, things were not going as planned at all!

Still, Simon (formerly known as Choppers, formerly known as Heathcliff Hodges) refused to ask his goon for a rescue. In his effort to become an evil mastermind, Simon had read many books, including one by business tycoon Donald Trump. It had argued that you should never let your underlings know that you need help. It undermined their respect for you. He would save himself.

He pulled himself to his feet and balanced precariously on

the tiny ledge. He searched the surface of the mountain for a handhold as he had done so many times before, and once again found nothing. Was he doomed to die? He went over everything he had ever been taught during his time as a secret agent. His former headquarters was filled to the brim with gadgets that would save his life—grappling guns, antigravity sneakers, and much more. But he'd have settled for a rope right then. He thought of his former teammates, especially Duncan Dewey, code name: Gluestick. Duncan would have had no problem with the icy cliffside. His skin produced a powerful adhesive that allowed him to stick to nearly any surface—hence his code name. He could walk along the ceiling like a fly or run up the side of a skyscraper.

It was all part of the upgrades the team members had received when they first became spies and members of an elite organization, the National Espionage, Rescue, and Defense Society, or NERDS, set with the task of saving the world from evil. Their fifth-grade weaknesses had been turned into superstrengths with the help of top-secret computer technology. Simon had huge front teeth, nearly as big as a horse's. It was how he had gotten his spy code name, Choppers. After his upgrades, he could use his buckteeth to hypnotize and control others. A lot of good that did now when he was alone and slowly turning into a snow cone. What had their hopelessly incompetent director, Agent Brand, said to the team? "You don't need gadgets. *You* are the gadgets." That was it! *Simon* was the gadget.

He slammed his face into the ice, driving his enormous front teeth deep into the mountain. Alternately using his teeth and the heavy cleated boots he wore, he began to climb slowly.

Perhaps Simon should have been grateful for his amazing upgrades and his many hours of training, but that wasn't how he felt. He was boiling mad. Sure, being a member of NERDS had been exciting, but because the work was secret, when the young spies weren't out on a mission they went right back to being picked on by their classmates. He and the others had suffered hundreds of wet willies, power wedgies, and flicked ears, but had they ever fought back? NO! They had to protect their secret identities and the work they did around the world. Well, it was all bunk! What was the point of having superpowers if you couldn't fight the bullies who tormented you? One day, while the school's resident meanie was dunking Simon's head into a toilet, the boy had realized that knuckleheads like this one would always torment people like him. The only way to change it would be to change everything. He decided to destroy the world. With society in shambles, people would be forced to rely on those with great intelligence—namely himself. Once again, reading and learning would be held in high regard, and people like Simon would be admired rather than abused and humiliated.

But his brilliant plan had been foiled by his own teammates.

Of all people in the world, he had been sure his former friends would join him. They too were misfits, outcasts, spazzes—they'd been bullied, stuffed in lockers, and forced to hand over their milk money on a daily basis. But Simon had failed to see the effect Duncan Dewey had on the others. The chubby kid had always been a walking ball of positive energy. The abuse he suffered time and time again seemed to roll right off his back. And his grating optimism had infected the team. He'd even managed to convince the others to accept Jackson Jones, one of their cruelest tormentors, as a new member. When Simon finally revealed his brilliant plan to the NERDS, Duncan turned against him and the others followed. They acted as if he had betrayed them!

Simon's thirst for revenge kept him going now through the painful climb. He was close to the summit. At the top, he hoped to find the remains of Dr. Jigsaw's secret fortress, or at least some clothing and food. But when he was only a few inches away, the mountain shook violently. He bit hard into the ice with what was left of his strength. He knew well the source of the tremors. Jigsaw's continental-shift machine was still active and was forcing the mountain farther into the sky. There was another quake, and this time Simon's teeth could not hold on. The next thing he knew, he was falling—down, down, down into the sea. He hit the waves with a painful splash and, exhausted, sank into the icy black abyss.

For Simon, death seemed inevitable. But fate had another

plan. It flash froze him like a fish stick. His heartbeat slowed to an almost undetectable rhythm, as did all his brain function. Every molecule in his body crystallized and a block of ice quickly formed around him, turning the boy into an ice cube of evil.

For weeks he floated south with the currents, bumping into ice floes around Iceland and Greenland, drifting past Canada and right down the eastern seaboard of the United States. Several lobster boats tried to reel him in, but the block was simply too heavy, and by the time Coast Guard officials got there to investigate, Simon had drifted away. The cube shrank a bit as it bobbed along in the warm waters of the Florida Keys, and on down past Cuba. Eventually, what was left of the chunk of ice washed ashore on a tiny, uninhabited island in the Caribbean Sea.

The waves hurled it onto a pebbly beach, where it was met by a squirrel with huge front teeth. Shocked by the cube's sudden appearance, the squirrel fled into the jungle and didn't return for three days. By then, the ice had melted considerably. When the squirrel mustered enough bravery, it hopped on top of the cube. It licked the ice and then spat out the salty water. Then, just as it was sure the ice posed no danger or benefit, it peered into the crystal cube and saw Simon's giant buckteeth. It let out a startled squeak and began to dig at the ice with its little claws. Its excited chirps brought dozens of squirrels out of the jungle, and together they scratched and chipped at the ice, working to free the boy. Squirrels are not big thinkers, as a rule, but if one had read the minds of these particular squirrels, one would understand that they thought they had stumbled upon their god.

Three months later . . .

High in the jungle trees, a dark figure jumped from limb to limb. It ran along impossibly narrow branches and leaped across insanely large gaps. As it hopped, it shook a feast of wild nuts from the branches down to a pack of squirrels waiting below. They scurried about, gathering the nuts, until a fight broke out between two of the bigger squirrels. There was much squeaking and screeching until the figure from above swooped down and landed in front of them. The squirrels suddenly lowered their heads, not from fear, but as if they were under a powerful spell. Their master had arrived.

He was not a squirrel, but a boy, with shaggy red hair and blue eyes, wearing torn jeans and broken shoes. His thick glasses were held together by tiny strips of sticky vines, and his two front teeth protruded out of his mouth like totem poles. He spoke: "None of you should be fighting over nuts. These are for the trip. If you want something to eat, work on the blackberry bush—the berries won't keep aboard the boat."

The boy pushed the hair out of his eyes and looked up. Black clouds were gathering in the east. He muttered, "If my calculations are correct, this entire island will be under water by

tomorrow night. Prepare yourselves, minions. We leave in the morning."

One of the little squirrels clicked and chirped.

"It doesn't matter where in this world we go, little one," Simon said. "For very soon I will have the entire planet in the palm of my hand."

It had taken Simon two months to construct his vessel. It was nothing fancy: a raft, a sail, and a makeshift cabin to shelter them when the waves were too strong. He knew a hurricane was coming. As part of his training as a member of NERDS, he had learned to read weather patterns, and this one indicated a particularly nasty storm.

The next morning, as the first cold drops of rain fell, he loaded the raft with the nuts they had been collecting for months, then marched his small army of squirrels aboard. Once they were settled, he gave his ship one final touch: With the juice of some blackberries, he painted a name on the side. Then, with all his strength, he shoved the raft into the water. The waves were rough and the squirrels squeaked in fear, but he ignored them. There was no turning back; the island offered them no hope anymore.

Who could say how long they were adrift? The bigger question was how they survived. The storm bullied the little boat, smashing it from left and right. It pounded on its hull while the thunder bellowed doom overhead, but still the tiny boat stayed upright.

When the hurricane finally passed, the danger wasn't over. The hot sun beat down mercilessly on the castaways. They drank the last of their fresh water. Soon, even the nuts were gone. Lying delirious on his battered raft, Simon prepared for his final hours. Then he felt a jolt; his little boat had hit dry land. He looked around. His squirrel crew shoved and pushed at one another for a better view. They had washed ashore on a rocky beach. Just beyond was a highway with cars zipping past in both directions.

"Where are we?" Simon said to himself. He saw buildings in the distance. One was a giant white tower rising high above everything. Simon recognized it at once and smiled. It was the Washington Monument. "We're home," he whispered.

The boy and his squirrels left their little ship on the shore of the Potomac and clambered up the embankment to the road. Simon turned and looked down at the tiny boat that had saved their lives. He smiled to see that the name he had painted on the side hadn't washed away. The *Revenge* had served its purpose.

Simon turned back to the highway and immediately stepped out into the path of a speeding Volkswagen Beetle.

The car came to a screeching stop only inches from Simon, and the angry driver leaped out, his face as red as a fire truck.

"Are you crazy, kid? That's how you get killed, you know. You can't just walk out into traffic. If I hadn't seen you and . . . hey! What's with all the squirrels?"

"Look at me, sir," Simon said.

The man tore his attention away from the army of furry rodents and eyed the boy. The kid looked as if he hadn't had a bath in a long, long time, but what was most interesting were his teeth. He had the biggest set of buckteeth the man had ever seen, and this particular man had grown up on a horse farm.

"We need a ride," Simon said as a strange fog came over the man. His eyes, fixed on Simon's teeth, glazed over and his jaw slackened.

"Sure," he said as if lost in thought. "Whatever you want."

Simon ordered the man back into his tiny car. Simon and the squirrels climbed in as well, and the boy directed the man to an address in nearby Arlington, Virginia.

On the way, they got a number of odd stares. A few people nearly drove off the road. It wasn't every day you saw a Volkswagen full of excited squirrels in the carpool lane.

Soon, the driver pulled up in front of a two-story Colonial home on a leafy green street in South Arlington. Simon told

45°13 N, 62°42 E

him to wait with the squirrels, and the boy snuck behind the house into the empty backyard. He scowled. Where was the swing set his father had built for him? Why would they take it down? Wouldn't his parents still hope he was coming back?

When he carefully peered in the window of his house and saw the spot on the wall that had once held his photograph, it dawned on him what had happened. The NERDS had erased his parents' memories and then removed all evidence that he had ever existed. After he disappeared, they wouldn't have wanted Simon's mother and father asking a lot of questions about his whereabouts. They couldn't risk the exposure of their secret society. Every agent knew that if he or she died on a mission, his or her very existence would be erased like dust from a chalkboard, but Simon had never thought it would happen to him.

Unfortunately, Simon's swing set had been more than a swing set. He raced to where it had once stood and got down on his hands and knees. He dug frantically in the ground. Just when he was about to give up, his fingers brushed against a tiny knob. He gave it a twist and a small portion of the yard lifted, revealing a compartment that held an odd collection of objects. Simon reached in, snatching a toothbrush and toothpaste, as well as a cell phone, a case of protein bars, and, finally, a black mask with a white skull painted on it. He closed the hole, turned the knob, and prepared to rush back to the car, then stopped. He had caught sight of his parents through the picture window. There they were, sitting together and reading the paper—his father working his way through the sports section, his mother busy with her real estate listings. Something inside Simon stirred. It hadn't been a bad life. In fact, his mother and father had tried hard with him. Suddenly, he wanted to rush in and demand that they remember him, but he fought the impulse. Someday, when he had conquered the world, he'd come back here. Someday . . .

He walked back to the car. The driver was starting to come out of his trance, so Simon flashed his choppers once more and got the man back under his control. He tossed the protein bars into the backseat, where the squirrels attacked them. He devoured two himself and then took out the toothpaste and toothbrush and snatched up one of his furry companions.

"This toothpaste will let you hypnotize people. It won't give you the same powers that I have—I've been upgraded by a supercomputer—but it will help you do what I just did to this driver for a short period of time."

The squirrel chirped as Simon started brushing its teeth.

"Why do you need the toothpaste?" Simon asked the squirrel. "Because if I'm going to take over the world, we need some spending money."

WELL, WELL, WELL—LOOK WHO'S BACK.
LONG TIME, NO SEE. I COULD HAVE SWORN
I'D SCARED YOU OFF WITH THE TEAM'S
SPINE-TINGLING ADVENTURE FROM THE
FIRST BOOK. MOST PEOPLE WHO READ IT
RAN HOME CRYING TO THEIR MOTHERS.
IT'S TRUE.
IT WAS ON THE NEWS!
BUT NOT YOU, HUH?
I GUESS YOU'RE MADE OF TOUGHER STUFF.
WE'LL SEE.

IN CASE YOU'VE FORGOTTEN, MY NAME IS
MICHAEL BUCKLEY. I'M A FORMER MEMBER
OF THE SECRET ORGANIZATION KNOWN

AS NERDS (THE NATIONAL ESPIONAGE, RESCUE, AND DEFENSE SOCIETY). LOTS OF FAMOUS PEOPLE HAVE BEEN MEMBERS OF THE TEAM. I CAN'T TELL YOU THEIR NAMES 'CAUSE THAT WOULD BLOW THEIR COVERS, BUT TRUST ME—THEY ARE OUT THERE. AND THEN THERE ARE A FEW OF US WHO STICK A LITTLE CLOSER TO HOME. I VOLUNTEERED TO DOCUMENT THE CURRENT TEAM'S MISSIONS AND HELP WEED THROUGH THE NEW RECRUITS EAGER TO JOIN. IF I REMEMBER CORRECTLY, YOU WERE INDUCTED INTO THE TEAM ON A TRIAL BASIS AND CHOSE A CODE NAME. GO AHEAD AND ENTER IT BELOW.

X_____ O⟍

REALLY?
THAT'S YOUR CODE NAME?
THAT'S ONE SILLY CODE NAME.

OK, OK, I'M SORRY I MADE FUN OF YOUR
CODE NAME. GEEZ, TOUCHY?
LET'S GET BACK TO BUSINESS. IT'S TIME
TO BECOME A FULL-FLEDGED NERD, BUT
BEFORE YOU START JUMPING UP AND
DOWN, YOU NEED TO KNOW THAT BEING A
SPY IS DANGEROUS. YOU COULD GET HURT,
KILLED, OR WORSE! SO READ THIS BOOK
FROM COVER TO COVER, AND IF YOU CAN
DO IT WITHOUT WETTING YOUR PANTS,
YOU MIGHT JUST HAVE A CHANCE . . .
BUT HONESTLY, MOST KIDS END UP
WITH SOGGY SHORTS. IT'S NOTHING
TO BE ASHAMED OF. . . .

WHO AM I KIDDING?
THAT'S TOTALLY EMBARRASSING!
MAYBE YOU SHOULD TAKE A QUICK TRIP
TO THE BATHROOM BEFORE YOU READ
THE NEXT SECRET FILE.

YOU BACK?
DID YOU WASH YOUR HANDS?
OK . . . PUT YOUR THUMB HERE.

LEVEL 1
ACCESS GRANTED

BEGIN TRANSMISSION:

1

38°53 N, 77°05 W

"Congratulations on stopping Professor Flurry and her deadly snow globe machine, Agent Gluestick," the Hyena said via a video chat. Her signal was breaking up and full of static, but nothing could dim the former beauty queen's bright green eyes.

"Just doing my job," the boy replied.

"Always the humble one, huh? I hear Braceface asked for a trophy and Wheezer wanted tickets to WrestleMania. Pufferfish asked for a case of anti-itch cream, and the other one—the hyper one?"

"Flinch."

"Yes, Flinch. He asked for something, but who can understand him? The boy talks a mile a minute."

"I only wish we could have saved Hollywood. When the doctor turned on her machine, it was sealed in a glass globe and rolled into the ocean."

"Eh, I was Ms. Preteen Hollywood, once. Trust me, it's not such a big loss."

"I heard you were on some secret mission."

The Hyena nodded. "Can't say much, only that it's warm. I was tired of the long johns and mittens. So much better working for the good guys. Though I wish I were a little closer to, you know . . ."

"Jackson?"

"If you tell, you're a dead man!" the Hyena cried. "Listen, the world needs saving so I gotta run. Tell the gang I said hi— oh, and next time I contact you on the video screen, would you mind standing on the floor instead of the ceiling? It's giving me motion sickness."

Duncan Dewey leaped down from the ceiling, landing squarely on the floor. "Sorry. Force of habit."

Suddenly there was a loud banging on the door across the room. "Hey, nerd! Open up!"

"Gotta run, too. Be careful, Mindy," Duncan replied.

The girl growled.

"Sorry. Be careful, Hyena," Gluestick said sheepishly.

Her face disappeared from the monitor just as a tiny blue orb floated out of a hole in the desk. It twittered as it buzzed around Duncan's head. Then it spoke in a rather dignified voice. "The Creature is at the door, Gluestick."

Duncan sighed. "I hear her, Benjamin."

"People in Boston can hear her," Benjamin replied. "Perhaps you should answer before she pounds the door down."

Duncan opened the door a crack. Outside was something so horrible, so disturbing, so nightmarish that it would have caused a grown man to scream in terror. It was Duncan's sister, Tanisha—or as Duncan and Benjamin called her, the Creature. The Creature was fuming mad. When she was angry, Duncan thought she resembled a pit bull sucking on a lemon. When she was happy? Well, he would say, imagine the same thing without the lemon.

"May I help you?"

"What are you doing in there?" the Creature snapped.

"I'm afraid that's classified."

Tanisha snarled. "More of your stupid secret agent stuff?"

"I could tell you, but then I'd have to kill you."

She growled. "Dad set fire to the house."

"Again?"

"Yes, again! Your crazy gadgets are impossible to use. I was nearly blasted through the bathroom window this morning using that stupid hair dryer you brought home."

"Perhaps it's not the hair dryer that is stupid but the person using it," Duncan mumbled.

"What did you say?" Tanisha cried as Duncan closed the door in her face.

The little blue orb darted up to him. "Time to put away the toys?"

Duncan nodded. "I'm afraid so, Benjamin. Activate bedroom mode."

At once the computer monitor disappeared into the ceiling, the desk flipped on its side and sank into the floor like a slice of bread into a toaster, and Duncan's leather chair rolled away behind the wall. When the room was empty, the walls themselves slid downward, revealing a curtained window, a dresser, a mirror, and a bookshelf stuffed with books about electronics and technology. A hole in the floor opened and a full-sized bed rose to the surface. The room's transformation was complete when a stack of *Popular Mechanics* magazines slid out from under the mattress.

"Now I need to get dressed for school, Benjamin," said Duncan. "Activate wardrobe mode."

"Of course," the orb replied as it spun like a top. Little blue light particles swirled around the room. They danced and twirled, combining into a three-dimensional hologram of a clothing store. Now standing before Duncan was another hologram—this was the human representation of the little blue orb: America's elder statesman Benjamin Franklin, who, like Duncan, had once been a spy. Benjamin was dressed in white stockings, breeches, and a long coat. He smiled as he pulled out a measuring tape and went about measuring Duncan's shoulder width, arm length, and inseam.

"How about something in a powdered wig?" Benjamin suggested, holding up a bright white hairpiece.

"Hmmm, maybe a little too eighteenth century?" Duncan replied.

Benjamin put the wig back, then presented a brown pinstripe suit. "Very well. This is pure twenty-first-century class. With a button-down shirt and a gray vest you would look very hip—like a young Frederick Douglass."

"No, I was thinking about the usual," the boy said.

Benjamin frowned. "The usual?"

Duncan nodded.

"Green shirt, purple pants, oxfords, all clashing?" Benjamin sighed.

Duncan nodded.

"OK." Benjamin and the store vanished, leaving just the blue orb floating in the air. It chirped and beeped, then panels on the bedroom walls slid back, revealing banks of red lasers. They scanned Duncan. His pajamas fell away with a flash as dozens of cables with mechanical hands on the ends dropped down from the ceiling. Each held a different tool: scissors, needles, thread, chalk, brushes, etc. When long swatches of thick, shiny, purple and green fabric unrolled from above, the hands went to work cutting and sewing the cloth into slacks and a shirt.

Within moments, the hands were finished and the small spy was squeezed into an eye-burning, ill-fitting outfit of clashing colors.

"Just how I like it," Duncan said as the orb floated onto his palm. He slipped it into his pants pocket and crept into the hallway. The Creature was waiting for him, her hands clenched into fists and her mouth twisted in a snarl.

"I heard what you said," she growled. "And now you're going to pay."

"You have to catch me first," Duncan said, leaping onto the wall and using his sticky hands and feet to scurry up to the ceiling. Tanisha ran after him, leaping up and swatting at him like he was a bug as he skirted the chandelier in the dining room and raced toward the kitchen. He managed to stay just out of reach, which made her all the angrier.

Luckily, Duncan's parents were waiting for him in the kitchen. A small but growing cloud of smoke was rising out of the toaster, and his father, Avery, dressed in work boots and overalls, was slapping at it with a dish towel. His mother, Aiah, looked on, urging his dad to calm down.

"Duncan!" said his mother when she spotted the boy. "What have I told you?"

"'No walking on the ceiling.' Sorry," Duncan said, and dropped to the floor. "So, I hear we have another five-alarm inferno in here."

Avery scowled at his son's joke.

"OK, no sense of humor this morning," Duncan said as he grabbed a remote control sitting on the kitchen counter. He punched in a series of numbers and a panel on the kitchen wall slid back. A tiny winged robot buzzed out carrying an even smaller fire extinguisher. It hovered over the toaster and blasted it with fire retardant until the flames were dead. Then the robot zipped back into its hidden compartment.

"Duncan, enough is enough!" Avery cried. "All the gadgets have to go! I feel like I'm trapped in a James Bond movie."

Aiah pursed her lips. "Avery, keep it down. We don't want the neighbors to hear. It's a national security thing!"

Avery frowned but lowered his voice. "When we agreed to let Duncan become a spy, I had no idea my house would be invaded by electronic doohickeys! Everything moves, beeps, and buzzes, and it's driving me crazy. All a man wants in the morning is an English muffin, but I need a degree in advanced engineering to use the toaster. Well, that's it. All of it has to go!"

"Dad, you can't be serious. All this tech makes our lives better. We have things here that no one else in the world will have for decades!" Duncan said.

"And all of it is obnoxious!"

"So is Duncan, but I don't hear anyone saying we need to toss him out with the trash," the Creature said.

"Tanisha!" his mother snapped.

Duncan ignored his sister. "Look, it's easy. Everything in the house can be controlled with this remote. First you push the yellow mounting button to activate the smart house system,

then you select the number of the device you want to use, and finally you push the green button to start. If you want to pull the shades down on the windows, it's yellow, then the number seven, then green."

Suddenly, the shades on the windows lowered, plunging the room into complete darkness. Duncan pressed the buttons that made the shades rise again.

"If you want ice, you press yellow, four, green." Ice tumbled out of the ice maker in the refrigerator door. "If you want coffee, you press yellow, nine, green." Suddenly, the coffee machine came to life, brewing a fresh pot of java. "If you want to change the wallpaper, you press yellow, seventeen, green." Suddenly, the floral-patterned wallpaper rolled up into the ceiling and was replaced with a jaunty nautical theme.

"All I want is an English muffin!" Avery cried.

"Simple. Yellow, forty-five, green, then you can select how well you want it toasted. You have seventeen options, from very light to very dark. When it's finished, the remote asks you for either butter or cream cheese and which of nine varieties of jams and jellies you like. I recommend number six: strawberry-peach preserves. It's crazy delicious."

"No! No! No! No! No!" Avery grabbed his thermos, lunch box, and coal-black half of an English muffin. He took a bite and grimaced. "We'll talk about this later. I've got to get to the garage. I've got three Pontiacs that need brakes and a Chrysler with a bad water pump."

"You aren't leaving this house without kissing me good-bye, are you?" Aiah said.

Duncan watched his dad's anger dissolve as he leaned down and kissed his wife on the cheek. Then he planted a kiss on the top of Duncan's head and gave Tanisha, standing in the doorway, a kiss on the forehead on his way out.

"Dad!" Tanisha complained. "I'm too old."

Avery rolled his eyes at his wife and darted out the door.

"If he would just read the manual," Duncan muttered. "It's really all self-explanatory."

"Duncan, honey, the manual is two thousand pages long," his mother said. "I don't want you to misunderstand. Your father is very proud of you and what you do for our country, but he didn't sign up to be a spy himself. Maybe you can leave some of your gadgets at school?"

"How about all of them?" the Creature quipped.

"Leave them at school?" Duncan exclaimed. "That's like telling me to leave my left leg at school, Mom."

"I hardly think that's the case," Aiah said as she filled two bowls full of cereal and milk. She added spoons, then steered her kids to the table. "We could get along without all the bells and whistles."

Duncan sat down and shoveled a spoonful of cereal into his mouth. He thought about what his mother had said as he looked around. The family's one-story ranch house was too small and had a leaky roof that required the strategic placement of buckets during heavy rains. The living room carpet looked like grass on an overused playground, and most of the furniture was so old, it should have been in a museum. They needed all the bells and whistles they could get.

Aiah gave her son a knowing look. "Duncan, we are doing just fine." Then she smiled. Duncan's mom had a smile that seemed to be borrowed from the sun. Duncan thought she was the most beautiful person in the world. If they could just bottle a little of the feeling he got when she grinned, they'd be millionaires ten times over. "I know you mean well, and some of these gadgets do make life a little easier, but take some advice from a person who has known your father for almost fourteen years. For a former boxer he's got a pretty even temper—it takes a lot to get him angry—but if you keep denying him his breakfast, you're going to see some of these gadgets getting a few right hooks and uppercuts. All he wants in the morning are smiles on our faces—" She stopped for a moment and flashed Tanisha a look.

"What?" the Creature said defensively.

Aiah continued, "*And* an English muffin. It's a *simple* pleasure, Duncan. I don't think we need the full budget of the United States government to make him some breakfast."

Duncan frowned. "I guess the RZ-481 Bread Warmer is out, then? It toasts both sides simultaneously using diamond-tipped lasers. It's state-of-the-art."

Aiah shook her head. "A ten-dollar toaster from the appliance store works just as well."

Duncan sighed. "Would you like me to ride a dinosaur to school while I'm at it?"

There was a honk outside.

"There's Aunt Marcella and you aren't finished eating. Hurry!"

Duncan cringed. Watching the Creature eat was enough to give a kid nightmares. There was so much crunching and grunting, you couldn't help feeling sorry for the cereal. He hopped up from his seat.

"Any big missions, today?" Aiah said as she gave him a hug. There was a hint of worry in her voice.

"Heaven forbid," the Creature said between bites. "If the world is dependent on chubby, we're all doomed."

Duncan ignored his sister and put on his jacket. "Sorry, Mom, but you don't have clearance high enough for that information. But I promise I'll be careful."

2

Albert Nesbitt was not a typical superhero. For one, he was not a muscle man with a steel jaw. In fact, he was five foot seven and easily a hundred and fifty pounds overweight. He had a bad complexion from eating too many snack cakes, and his long, stringy red hair hung down his face like wet ivy. He was also thirty-seven years old.

He had no superpowers to speak of, either. He was not faster than a speeding bullet. He was not more powerful than a locomotive. He could not leap tall buildings in a single bound. He could barely hop out of a chair.

He also lacked a secret headquarters. He had no Hall of Justice, no Fortress of Solitude, no Batcave. All he had was his mother's basement, which contained a rather funky smelling recliner, empty bags of cheese puffs, laundry stacked waist-high, a leaky inflatable mattress, old pizza boxes, an exercise bike where he hung his shirts, and a ping-pong table with no paddles.

But he did have a couple things going for him. He had a supercomputer—hand-built from discarded computers he rescued from the town's landfill. Albert had a knack for seeing how things worked and improving on them. His computer was the fastest in the country.

The other thing he had that all do-gooding superheroes need was a secret identity. You see, Albert Nesbitt, thirty-seven-year-old shut-in, living in his mother's basement, was also the shadowy nightstalker of the Internet known as Captain Justice. From his recliner he surfed the Web looking for computer-based crime. So far, he had stopped a gang of international ATM bandits and put down a Nigerian credit card scam without leaving his basement. Sure, swooping in through a window and punching a criminal in the jaw sounded great, but Albert had to be practical. He wasn't in the kind of shape to smash through a window, and until he finally kept his New Year's resolution and signed up for that membership at Owen's Muscle House Gym, he'd continue to lurk in cyberspace, stopping electronic crime wherever it reared its ugly head. The downside, unfortunately, was that the bad guys never got to see his supercool costume: a black-and-green latex getup complete with boots, gloves, cape, and mask. There was even an arrow-shaped cursor on his chest.

Now his computer buzzed with activity. The security system of a nearby bank had been breached and a silent alarm had been tripped. But by the time Albert pinpointed the location of the bank, the alarm was turned off again. Odd. Albert turned on the police radio he had bought at a recent auction. He heard someone announce that a police presence was not necessary at the bank. It was a 431. This was police code for a false alarm.

Still, something seemed off. With a few keystrokes, Albert hacked into the bank's main server. Soon, he had taken control of the bank's security cameras, and what he saw was very strange indeed. A child with enormous buckteeth was robbing the bank . . . with the help of a team of squirrels. The furry felons were holding out sacks as frightened tellers filled them with cash. The bank's security guards stood by, watching the whole event without lifting a finger to help. Albert had never seen anything like it, but he knew one thing for sure—this was a job for Captain Justice. He unplugged his phone and hooked it into the back of his computer. He pressed a button that linked the phone to the Internet, then pushed another to scramble the signal in case anyone might be tracing his call. Then he dialed 911.

"Nine-one-one. What's your emergency?" the operator said.

"Hi, I'm at South Arlington National Bank and it's being robbed," he said. He could hear the faint clicking on the line that told him he was right to be worried. The police were trying

to trace the call. Albert told them everything he saw on the cameras and hung up. Five minutes later, he watched the boy throw down his bag of money and gather his hairy gang. They ran out of the bank moments before the police stormed inside. The robber had escaped, but Captain Justice had foiled the crime.

Feeling proud, Albert turned off his computer and spent the next twenty-five minutes trying to get out of his costume. Latex had been a bad idea.

When he was in his street clothes at last, he climbed the basement stairs to the kitchen. Mama was cutting coupons at the table. She was a short, stocky woman who wore high heels and tons of gold jewelry at all times—even to bed. She had a bun of red hair and smelled of cabbage soup. When Albert saw her, he forced a smile, then turned and locked the padlock on the basement door.

"Good to see you have returned to the land of the living," Mama said. "You know it's nearly eleven thirty."

Albert frowned. Mama could be very critical. "I'm going out."

"Where?" she cried.

"Big Planet."

Mama produced an orchestra of sighs. "More of those stupid funny books?"

"They're called graphic novels, Mama."

Mama rolled her eyes. "They're called a waste of time."

Albert didn't argue with her. He had done something good that day. He was a real hero and he didn't want his mother to ruin it for him, so he kissed her on the cheek and headed outside.

"Be back by six. We're having cabbage soup for dinner and it's no good cold," she said.

"It's no good hot," Albert said under his breath as he rushed out the back door. He was soon whizzing down the sidewalk on his rusty red scooter to the taunts of the children in the neighborhood. Albert didn't care about their hurtful insults. It was comic book day at Big Planet and comic book day was his favorite day of the week.

Big Planet Comics was a world of *Pows! Zaps!* and *Bangs!* Every shelf was the home of good guys and bad guys—all in full color. There were war comics, superhero comics, horror comics, sci-fi comics, romance comics. There were comics based on classic novels like *Moby-Dick* and *Heart of Darkness,* and even comic book versions of the lives of Jesus and Buddha. And that wasn't all. Big Planet had everything a fanboy could ever want—action figures, posters, games, toys, scale models, replicas, T-shirts, and most importantly, people, just like him. When Albert stepped through the doors of the shop, he was surrounded by people who loved, lived, ate, and breathed comics. These were his people.

But that day there was a black cloud over Big Planet. A strange man lurked among the shelves. He had slicked-back hair and a nose that looked as if it had been slapped around by a hockey stick. His arms were as thick as railroad ties, and on his left hand, or rather, lack of one, was a silver hook. He looked as if somewhere there was a comic book missing its villain.

Not that the people inside the shop would reject someone because of his appearance. What turned them off about the brute was how he manhandled the comics. He bent them. He smeared them with his greasy hand. He scratched them with his hook. He was single-handedly turning mint-condition comics into "fair condition"—at best.

"Heroes disgust me," the man grunted at Albert. His voice sounded like a sledgehammer.

Albert tilted his head but said nothing.

"They offer so little to the world," the man continued.

"If you're into books about villains there are plenty—"

The man continued as if Albert had not spoken. "Do they build things? Do they invent things? Do they create machines that change the world? No! All heroes do is break things."

"That's a little simple," Albert said.

The man turned to him and frowned. "Oh, is it? Look at the covers of these books. Every single one of them has a scientist, an inventor, a visionary whose plans are ruined by a man in rubber pajamas. These so-called heroes hate science. They turn their fists and powers on great thinkers. Heroes are a menace. Don't ya agree, Albert?"

"How did you know my name?" Albert said.

"I know lots of stuff about you, Albert. Or do you prefer your other name, Captain Justice?"

Albert felt a bead of sweat trickle down his face. How did this man know his secret identity? The same thing had happened to Spider-Man once, but for the life of him Albert could not remember how Peter Parker had handled it. "What do you want?" he whispered.

"Me? Nuthin'. It's my boss. He wants to meet you," the man said as he handed Albert a business card. It was stuck on the end of his hook. "He wants your help. If you're interested, go to the address on the card."

Albert gingerly pulled the card off the sharp tip. "My help? What can I do for him?"

"He wants to hire you to do a job for him and he's offering you your greatest desire as payment."

"And how would he know what my greatest desire is?" Albert asked as he looked down at the card. The name Simon was printed on it. The goon's hook had cut a hole in the center of the "o."

"Isn't it obvious, pal? You want to have superpowers—real-life superpowers."

3

38°53 N, 77°05 W

"Good afternoon," Duncan said to a stocky, thick-limbed lunch lady behind the counter in the school cafeteria. She had hairy, tattooed arms and smoked a cigar. She also needed a shave.

The lunch lady nodded. "Good afternoon," she said in a gruff voice. "I have something very special on the menu that I think you—"

Duncan shook his head and lifted a brown paper bag so the lunch lady could see. "I brought mine from home. I just need a spoon, please."

The lunch lady bit down on his lower lip. He took great pride in his cooking. Yes, I said "he."

The lunch lady had a few secrets besides his carefully guarded recipes. Most of them are classified, but suffice it to say the lunch lady was not really a lunch lady. Nor was the lunch lady really a *lady*. No, she—I mean *he*—was actually a spy, just like Duncan

Dewey. But while Duncan got to stroll the halls of Nathan Hale Elementary dressed as a normal fifth grader, the lunch lady had to wear a smock, wig, and hairnet to work every single day. Still, despite his lousy cover, he was content. He had discovered the joy of cooking. It wasn't as much fun as, say, cleaning his bazooka or knife-fighting with terrorists, but it did give him some satisfaction.

"Are you sure? Today we have tilapia with cranberries and capers," he continued. "Tilapia is a lovely fish—"

Duncan shook his head. "I'm good. Just the spoon, please."

The lunch lady frowned and eyed Duncan's sack lunch with disdain. "You eat too much of that stuff, kid. Don't you ever get tired of it?"

Duncan shook his head as the lunch lady handed him his utensil. "How could I get tired of the most delicious thing in the world?"

The lunch lady waved the boy away. "Then go! Get out of my kitchen!" he bellowed.

In the lunchroom, Duncan quickly spotted his best friend, Flinch. Flinch was a scrawny Mexican-American kid with dark hair and eyes. Like Duncan, he brought his own lunch. In Flinch's case, two huge chocolate bars stacked like a sandwich with fruit pies and candy corn between them. As a side he had two perfectly toasted balls of fried ice cream, and for dessert, a jar of Marshmallow Fluff. He inhaled all of it at an incredible speed, and within a few seconds the boy was hooting and bouncing in his chair like a monkey.

"The lunch lady is grouchy," Duncan said.

Flinch opened his mouth and a stream of crazy words and noises that made no sense spilled out. There were a few high-pitched screams and he slammed his head into the tabletop a couple times, then giggled like an idiot. Finally, he reached inside his shirt and turned a big glowing knob counterclockwise. It seemed to calm him down.

"Sorry, I'm a little wound up today," Flinch said.

"Just today, huh?" Gluestick asked with a smile. He had known Flinch for almost two years, and he had always been hyperactive. Luckily, when the boys became members of NERDS, Flinch was given a special harness that channeled all that sugary energy into superhuman strength and speed. The harness also helped calm him down when he was on the verge of a hyperactive fit. Without it he was practically a blur of nervousness—hence his nickname, Flinch.

"Where's the rest of the team?" Duncan said.

"Last I saw, Brett Bealer was 'escorting' them into the bathroom for their daily dip into the toilet," Flinch said. "They'll be along as soon as they dry their hair."

"Any word from Agent Brand or Ms. Holiday?" Duncan asked as he opened his own sack lunch and took out his feast: a bologna sandwich, a banana, a small container of raisins, and a bottle of Elmer's Glue. He opened the cap on the glue and smelled it the way grown-ups sniff a glass of wine. His nose came alive with flavors. It had been a good year for craft adhesives. Still, he knew he shouldn't eat his dessert first, so he put the cap back on and set it aside.

"Nothing yet," Flinch said. "I did run into Brand this morning, but he's still in a foul mood. He wouldn't even talk to me."

"Ms. Holiday told me he's still very upset about Heathcliff's betrayal of the team. She says he thinks he failed us by not seeing what was going on earlier."

Flinch shook his head. "I've known Heathcliff since the first grade. I didn't see it coming. He was just a bad box of graham crackers."

Suddenly, Duncan felt a tingle in his nose. His eyes watered and he let out a loud and obnoxious sneeze. Flinch did the same and then both of the boys heard a familiar voice inside their heads. "Gluestick, Flinch, this is Ms. Holiday. We need you in the Playground at once."

Flinch hopped up, pounded on his chest, and bellowed like Tarzan. "Finally, a mission. I thought we were going to have to spend the day in class!"

"On our way," Duncan said out loud, causing several children at nearby tables who had not heard the voice to move farther away.

Together Duncan and Flinch dashed out of the cafeteria. They weaved in and out of other students, slinked past the suspicious eyes of Principal Dehaven, and zipped down the halls as fast as they could. Along the way they came across a trio of children hurrying in the same direction. The first was Jackson Jones—a wide-eyed kid with lots of product in his blond hair and the worst set of braces ever attached to a human being. The second was Matilda Choi—a tiny Korean-American girl whose asthma inhalers never left her hands. And last was Ruby Peet, a rail-thin girl with a poof of blond hair and thick glasses. She spent most of her days scratching and avoiding the millions of things she was allergic to. At the moment her hands were swollen to the size of balloons.

"It's bad news," she said. "I know it's bad news."

"How can you tell?" Duncan asked.

"I'm allergic to bad news," she said, showing him her hands.

Jackson shrugged. "Agent Brand probably wants to lecture us again about filing our reports."

Matilda rolled her eyes and dashed out of the way of a group of giggling kindergartners. "I highly doubt he would call us in for paperwork."

"He would if you hadn't filed any since you became an agent," Jackson said with a mischievous grin.

Matilda laughed, but when she spotted Ruby's disapproving look, she forced a frown onto her face. Ruby still wasn't thrilled to have Jackson as part of the NERDS team. He had once been a bully—until he got his braces—and was a bit too arrogant for his own good.

"I hope it's a mission," Duncan said. "There are some new gadgets I want to try out."

"Who cares about gadgets?" Matilda said. "I just hope I get to bodyslam someone."

They rounded the corner and came to a dead stop. Blocking their path was a pack of bullies, led by Brett Bealer, Jackson's former best friend.

"Well, well, well," Brett said. "If it isn't the nerd herd. What are you doing in my halls, losers?"

"These aren't your halls!" Ruby cried.

The outburst caused Brett's gang to circle the children, like a pack of jackals searching for weaknesses.

"Gluestick! Where are you and the rest of the team?" Ms. Holiday's voice sounded in Duncan's head. "Agent Brand is in a particularly grumpy mood this afternoon. Don't keep him waiting."

"On our way," Duncan mumbled. Then he turned to Brett. "He's right, Ruby. We have no business wandering around like we belong here. I think we need to be taught a lesson."

"What?" Matilda cried.

"Duncan, you're taking the nice guy thing a bit too far," Jackson added.

Brett scratched his head as if he had just opened a ten-thousand-piece jigsaw puzzle and had no idea what picture the pieces would make.

"Maybe you should stuff us into these lockers," Duncan said, pointing to a row of lockers nearby.

"Oh, I get it," Jackson said, giving the chubby boy a knowing wink. "Yeah, that will teach us!"

"Good idea, nerd! Get 'em, guys," Brett said. Duncan and his friends were roughly grabbed by the arms, necks, and underwear waistbands and shoved unceremoniously into lockers. Then the doors were slammed shut.

Now, for ordinary kids, getting stuffed in a locker would be the worst humiliation ever, but Duncan, Flinch, Ruby, Matilda, and Jackson were no ordinary kids and these were no ordinary lockers. A blue light flashed in the ceiling of Duncan's locker and a robotic female voice could be heard.

"Welcome, agents. Prepare for transport to the Playground."

The floor disappeared beneath Duncan, and the chubby boy was spun, shot, flipped, flopped, twisted, and turned through a series of tubes, shafts, and loop-the-loops until he finally plopped into a leather chair at the center of a huge subterranean chamber.

All around him in the cavernous room were scientists in white lab coats, working on complicated experiments that pushed the limits of imagination: robotic pets, exploding lunch boxes, sneaker silencers, even a new underwater breathing prototype called Scuba Gum. No wonder they called the place the Playground. To Duncan it was heaven on earth—filled with cool inventions and brilliant people who loved science and technology as much as he did. He would have to leave NERDS when he turned eighteen, but he was already considering a job working here as a researcher when he retired.

The rest of the team arrived, landing in their own leather

chairs. They were seated at a glass table made up of thousands of wires, circuits, and blinking lights. At its center was a hole. Duncan reached into his pocket and removed the blue orb he called Benjamin. It floated out of his palm and hovered over the hole.

"Let's get started," said a voice from behind the kids. They turned to find a tall man in a tuxedo. His name was Alexander Brand, and at one time he had been America's greatest secret agent—dashing, fearless, staggeringly handsome. He was the man the government called when no one else could get the job done. But then he had been injured in the line of duty and forced to use a cane to get around; his life as a spy had come to an abrupt halt. Still, his mind was as dangerous as his body had once been, so he was the perfect person to become Director of the National Espionage, Rescue, and Defense Society, though it was clear to Duncan and the others the man wasn't completely comfortable managing a group of fifth-grade superspies.

Duncan was incredibly curious about Brand. He was a mystery. Duncan had used Benjamin to try to track down information about him but had found nothing. There were no clues to how he had been injured, where he grew up, or even the names of his mother and father. It was as if the man did not really exist, and though Duncan was tempted to hack into Brand's government file, he knew the former spy would be furious if he discovered the breach. He was not the kind of man who liked to share. In fact, he spoke very little, unless, of course, he was angry, which was frequently.

"So, boss, what's the trouble—"

Brand raised his hands to silence Ruby. "Heathcliff Hodges."

The children looked at one another in stunned silence.

"He's back," Brand said.

"That's not possible," Ruby said. She began to feverishly scratch her leg. She was allergic to impossibilities.

"Pufferfish is right," Jackson replied. "I saw him fall into the ocean. There's no way he could have survived."

"Apparently, no one told Heathcliff," their director said. "Benjamin, could you be so kind as to replay the bank footage we received?"

The blue orb hovered on the glass table before them. It let out a few odd chirps and suddenly a dozen television monitors lowered from the ceiling and flickered to life. The screens showed a young boy in a black mask with a white skull on it using a herd of squirrels to empty cash drawers. The boy took off his mask to reveal his enormous teeth. Duncan watched the security guards and Heathcliff's hostages suddenly calm down, then follow his commands like sheep.

"Aarakdhgyyg!" Flinch said, then turned a knob on his harness. "Sorry, too much sugar at lunch. How many banks has he robbed?"

"This is his fifth heist," another familiar voice said. From one of the passages came a stunning woman with blond hair and blue eyes. She wore a cashmere sweater and a wool skirt. Stylish glasses sat on the end of her button nose. Ms. Holiday was the school's librarian, but she was also the team's information specialist. "We estimate that he's stolen nearly a hundred thousand dollars so far, focusing on the tellers. He also hypnotizes the customers into using their ATM cards to empty their accounts."

"Why not head for the vaults?" Matilda said. "That's where most of the money is kept."

"Modern bank security systems make the vaults nearly impenetrable. They've made a guard with a nightstick obsolete," Ms. Holiday said.

Duncan had read a lot about banks in magazines and books. He was fascinated with how their security systems worked. He spoke up. "Even if Simon were to break into a vault, he would find a steel wall blocking his exit, then sleeping gas knocking him out until the cops could arrest him. If he managed to get past all that, many banks have a program that drops the vault into a chamber dozens of feet below the ground, making it nearly impossible to escape."

"What do you think that little runt wants with the money?" Matilda asked.

Jackson shook his head. "It's not about the money."

"Then what?" Ruby said.

"Attention," Jackson said. No one challenged him. Braceface was an expert on getting attention, having once been the most popular kid at Nathan Hale Elementary. "If you're trying to be inconspicuous, you don't rob a bank with a herd of squirrels. He wants us to see him. He wants us to know he's still alive and plotting something new."

END TRANSMISSION.

YOU'RE BACK.
GOOD.
NOW LET'S START TRAINING
YOU FOR YOUR LIFE AS A
SECRET AGENT. WHAT? YOU
WANT TO KNOW WHEN YOU GET
TO LEARN THE COOL STUFF.
YOU MEAN LIKE JUMPING OUT
OF A BURNING PLANE, FIRING
A BAZOOKA WHILE RIDING A
JET SKI, AND KNOCKING A BAD
GUY OUT WITH A KARATE CHOP
TO THE NECK? WHOA . . . SLOW
DOWN THERE, BUDDY. FIRST,
LET'S FOCUS ON A BASIC SKILL
EVERY SPY MUST KNOW: THE
ABILITY TO READ AND WRITE
SECRET MESSAGES.

SOUNDS EASY, HUH?
WE'LL SEE. THIS IS
A LITTLE SOMETHING
WE CALL THE ALPHABET.

ABCDEFGHIJKLMNOPQRSTUVWXYZ

HOPEFULLY, YOU RECOGNIZE
IT. AND THIS IS A LITTLE
SOMETHING WE CALL
A CIPHER CODE.

TDNUCBZROHLGYVFPWIXSEKAMQJ

EACH LETTER IN THE
ALPHABET CORRESPONDS TO
THE LETTER IN THE CIPHER
CODE PRINTED BENEATH IT.

ABCDEFGHIJKLMNOPQRSTUVWXYZ
TDNUCBZROHLGYVFPWIXSEKAMQJ

SO I'M GOING TO SEND
YOU A VERY SENSITIVE
AND SECRET MESSAGE
WRITTEN IN CIPHER CODE.
THEN IT'S YOUR JOB TO
TRANSLATE IT INTO OUR
ALPHABET. YOU READY?
AGAIN, THIS MESSAGE
IS JUST FOR YOU.

SRC XYCGG FB QFEI BCCS OX YTLOVZ YC NIQ.

The smell of your
feet is making me cry.

LISTEN, SOMEBODY HAD TO
SAY SOMETHING. YOU CAN'T
BE A SPY WITH THAT KIND
OF FUNK. THE BAD GUYS
WILL SMELL YOU
A MILE AWAY.

OH, GOOD JOB ON THE
CIPHER, TOO . . . STINKY.

LEVEL 2

ACCESS GRANTED

BEGIN TRANSMISSION:

4

Albert looked down at the business card. Then he looked up at the abandoned entrance of the South Arlington Botanical Garden. The garden had been closed to all but vermin for nearly a decade. Albert had visited many times as a child. The place had once been glorious, but now was overgrown and wild. Someone had vandalized the gate, pulling it off its hinges and leaning it against a wall. Anyone could walk inside.

"This can't be the place," Albert said. He looked at the business card once more. There was no mistake.

He wondered if he was the victim of some elaborate hoax. There were people at Big Planet Comics whom he would call rivals. He had once gotten into a heated conversation with Ivan Purlman about whether Dick Grayson, Jason Todd, or Tim Drake was the better Robin to Bruce Wayne's Batman. Could Ivan have decided to teach him a lesson by concocting this silly prank?

Albert always had trouble making friends, and his mama was to blame—Mama and her stupid plans. When he was just three months old, his mama had made a chart that plotted out his entire life. Some of the highlights were: winning the National Spelling Bee at age ten; going to Space Camp at fourteen; early admission into an Ivy League college at sixteen; graduating with a full doctorate by twenty-one; and at twenty-five, marrying a woman she introduced him to, followed by lots and lots of grandbabies.

She planned for every possible obstacle and even allotted for a short puberty-fueled struggle for independence when he was fifteen. She figured Albert would need only a couple of weeks before he came to his senses and realized he should put all his faith in his mama.

How her little baby would get to such personal success was a little hazy, so she paid close attention to what the other mothers on the block were planning for their children. Tommy Beacon's father was pushing his son on the swings and toward a career as a marine biologist. Nikki Mock's mother was laying the groundwork for her daughter to be appointed as Secretary of Education. Mark Killian's parents had their son sleeping with a catcher's mitt. Mama knew she had better decide quickly before all the good careers were snapped up, so after much debate she decided that Albert would be a brilliant scientist, and because she loved him so much, she set about brainwashing her son into doing just that.

Each night, when Albert was ready for a good-night story, Mama would forgo *Harry the Dirty Dog* and *Where the Wild Things Are* in favor of Einstein's theory of relativity or the latest article on climate change. She emptied his room of toys and filled it with alkaline test strips, microscopes, and fossils. She hung the periodic table of the elements on his wall and made a mobile for his crib featuring her favorite igneous rocks.

Holidays were just another opportunity to immerse the boy in his would-be career. Every Christmas, Albert would wake up early to find Santa had left a Bunsen burner or a petri dish filled with molds under the tree. On Easter, instead of searching for eggs, Albert hunted for test tubes that Mama had hidden throughout the yard. Halloween was a chance to dress up as different kinds of scientists. At seven Albert was a paleontologist carrying around a plastic dinosaur bone. At ten he went as a mineralogist dragging a lump of quartz from house to house. At twelve he went "trick-or-sleeting" as a meteorologist. It didn't seem to matter to Mama that each year her son's costume was nearly identical to the previous year's.

By Albert's thirteenth birthday, Mama finally realized what her son's true calling was—computer science. Her revelation had nothing to do with anything he had mentioned or hinted at. In fact, Albert had shown very little interest in computers, but his mother saw the kind of money a computer mogul made and gave her son a laptop computer for his birthday.

Much to Mama's great satisfaction, Albert was immediately hooked. Within a matter of months, he knew everything there was to know about the machine—the bits and bytes, the boards and binaries. Soon he had taken his computer apart and rebuilt it to make it not only more efficient, but also incredibly powerful.

Mama couldn't have been happier. She sat back and marveled at her cunning, wondering if perhaps she should write a book on making young boys into successful men. Unfortunately, Mama's dream was soon to wither. Despite all her careful planning, she was unprepared for the distraction that would ruin everything. It wasn't girls—the poor boy was a physical mess who rarely saw the sunshine, let alone a girl's approving gaze. It wasn't cars. She had seen dozens of mothers lose their sons to hot rods and motorcycles, and wouldn't allow auto magazines past the door. No, the thing that brought her house of cards crashing down around her was comic books. At the age of fifteen, a neighbor lent Albert a copy of *The Amazing Spider-Man* #159. Albert read it cover to cover, then read it again. And again. And again. And again. Mama gave it little attention at first. After all, she had noticed that the issue he was reading contained a character known as Doctor Octopus. He had a PhD. Mrs. Octopus must have been very, very proud.

Unfortunately, Spider-Man was just the beginning of Albert's obsession. When he returned the well-worn comic to his friend, he was told he would have to buy his own from then on out. He promptly went home and took a hammer to his piggy bank, which was stuffed with money for college, and squandered Mama's dreams on Batman, the Green Lantern, the Incredible Hulk, the Fantastic Four, the X-Men, the Avengers, and of course, Superman. Albert read everything his local comic shop sold and spent his weekends at garage sales patrolling for back issues of Sgt. Rock and golden age Justice League. And quite soon, Doctor Octopus, as well as Doctor Fate, Doctor Doom, and Doctor Strange, were taking up more space in his imagination than Dr. Nesbitt—future computer scientist.

Mama was horrified. If her son did not grow up to run a multinational software corporation, what would she brag about with Linda Caruso from next door? Linda had been preparing her son for a career as a lawyer, dressing him in pinstriped suits and taking him to wine country on vacations. If Albert didn't give up his ridiculous love of funny books, Linda would look down her nose at Mama forever! Something drastic had to be done.

So, one day, when Albert was at school, she packed up his comic book collection and put it on the curb. As she watched the garbage men toss the boxes into the back of their truck, she told herself she was doing her son a favor. One day, when he was flying around the world in his private jet, he would thank her.

When Albert got home from school and realized what she

had done, he got on his scooter and tore through town until he tracked down the garbage truck that had stolen his treasures.

The next day, after rescuing his collection out of a landfill, he moved all his belongings down into the basement and had a locksmith install tamper-proof deadbolts on the door. Mama's relationship with him was never the same. They rarely spoke except at mealtimes. More than twenty years later he was still down there. What he was doing, Mama could not say, but she gave up on his career in science when she found his microscopes in the trash can.

Despite his appearance and his rather smelly secret lair, Albert was not lazy. He had put his scientific training to good use. He had conducted hundreds, thousands of experiments with a single aim: to acquire real superpowers. He'd bombarded spiders with radiation in hopes of gaining their abilities, landing in the hospital instead. He had poured toxic waste on himself in hopes of enhancing his senses, and ended up being scrubbed with wire brushes by men in hazmat suits. He'd even tried to build a flying suit out of iron, only to trap himself inside for several days.

Now, as he stood in front of the abandoned garden with its rusting gate and potholed parking lot, he debated with himself. Should he turn away from almost certain ridicule, or should he listen to the rhythmic knocking of destiny? He chose destiny and entered the botanical garden.

It was a jungle inside. With no one to manage them, the trees were taking the grounds back, slowly erasing the park from existence and returning it to forest. They had grown tightly together, their branches intertwining and creating a lush green canopy that blocked out the sun. Many of the buildings had trees growing out through their windows and roofs. Leaves were scattered everywhere.

Suddenly, a rope ladder fell from the trees above, almost knocking Albert in the head. Albert looked up to find out who had nearly killed him and saw the man he had met at the comic shop. He was looking down at him from what appeared to be a huge tree house.

"The boss is waiting," the goon said.

"The boss is up there?" Albert said, eyeing the rope ladder with doubt.

The goon nodded. "And he doesn't like to wait."

Albert frowned but hoisted himself onto the ladder. He climbed the best he could, but it wasn't easy. He grunted and puffed, occasionally whining, until he got to the top, where the goon helped him stand. What he saw shocked him. Stretching out for acres was a palace formed from the trees' intertwining limbs. They had created a floor firm enough to stand on, and there was furniture too, made from both plant life and stuff you would find in a store—including a refrigerator, a microwave, and beds. And everywhere Albert looked there were squirrels—dozens of them, leaping from tree to tree as they patched holes in the branches with trash and leaves. They were building a nest—only on a gigantic scale.

"Boss," the brute called out, ignoring Albert's bewilderment.

Suddenly, a spotlight appeared, shining on a small figure wearing a skull mask. He was sitting in a high-backed chair, enjoying a bowl full of nuts. He had lifted his mask up just enough so that he could eat, revealing two gigantic front teeth, like posts on a white picket fence. Albert could not take his eyes off of them.

"Albert Nesbitt, it's good to meet you," the masked figure said between bites. His voice was young—that of a boy. "I am Simon."

Albert eyed the figure closely. "You're just a kid."

The squirrels seemed to sense his disrespect. They leaped at him and scratched at his face and hands. He fell to the floor, screaming for mercy.

"Minions!" Simon shouted, and the squirrels scurried back to his chair. "Please forgive them. They are very protective of me. After all, you've caused me a great number of headaches recently. You've been meddling in my affairs, Albert."

Albert knew at once the boy was talking about the bank robbery. He was preparing to run when the goon clamped a giant hand on Albert's shoulder. Albert couldn't move an inch.

The boy smiled. "Welcome to my secret lair. It's just

temporary. As soon as I have the funds I will build something a little more permanent and with a lot fewer termites. For now, it's the perfect hiding place and it keeps my friends happy." One of the squirrels hopped on to the boy's shoulder and twittered something in his ear. The boy laughed as if he had just heard a hilarious joke.

"What do you want with me?"

"Relax, there's no need for hysterics. If I wanted to harm you, my associate would have already taken care of that," the

boy said. "Look, we're getting off on the wrong foot, and I'm such a big fan of yours."

"A fan of mine? Why?"

"Well, maybe the word *fan* is not appropriate. You are a mess, really, but your brain—that amazing brain of yours . . . It takes someone of great intellect to stop me, and you managed to do it with a computer you built in your mother's basement."

"I have a way with computers," Albert said modestly.

"I know, and it's a talent that could prove very useful to me. I'd like to hire you, Albert. I want you to build something for me with that amazing brain of yours, and I can pay you very well. My friend informed you of what I'm offering—correct?"

"He said you could give me superpowers," Albert said, eyeing the big man for traces of a lie.

"That is true. I have access to a machine that can take your weaknesses and turn them into strengths. With the great number of weaknesses you possess, you could be turned into an incredibly powerful individual. You could become a real superhero, Albert. Though, I hope you will give some thought to a career in supervillainy. It can be quite rewarding."

A television monitor mounted on a tree came to life with a fuzzy image. "I'd like to show you something," Simon continued as the image came into focus. Albert wasn't exactly sure what he was seeing. It looked like thousands of electronic bees scurrying about in a strange, light-filled hive. He studied them, then realized what he was seeing: not living creatures, but tiny robots. The longer he looked, the wider his mouth opened.

"Are those—"

"Nanobytes," Simon said.

Albert stammered, "Scientists have been developing those for over a decade, but what you have here is way beyond the current science. How? Where?"

"All will be revealed in time. And, anyway, wouldn't you prefer to know what they do?"

Albert smiled. He liked mysteries, especially ones involving computers.

The image zoomed out until the little robots were smaller and smaller and smaller. When the camera stopped, all Albert could see was a set of huge buckteeth.

"Those things are in your mouth?" Albert cried.

Simon laughed. "Yes, they have been implanted into my two front teeth. They create a hallucinogenic phenomenon that makes people susceptible to hypnotic suggestions."

"So it's mind control! You control people's minds with your teeth!"

Simon nodded. "The ability has been further supercharged by a hallucinogenic toothpaste. Combined with my incredible charm and good looks—"

Albert interrupted him. "If you can control people, what do you need me for? All you have to do is flash those big teeth and people will do whatever you say. Everything you could ever want is at your fingertips."

"Not everything, my new friend. The nanobytes cannot give me revenge. You see, there's a certain boy in this town with technology similar to mine and I'd like to destroy him."

"Why not send this guy?" Albert said, pointing to the goon.

"What fun would that be? I'd rather make him doubt himself and the things he holds dear. You see, my friend, it is not fists or superpowers that destroy a man, it's self-doubt. Albert, you are going to help me destroy this boy, and when he is destroyed you will get your superpowers."

"Has this kid committed a crime? Is he a bad person?"

Simon shook his head. "Actually, he's really very nice."

"But if I help you destroy him, that would make me a villain."

Simon nodded.

Albert searched his brain for other superheroes who had started out as villains before they turned to a life of fighting crime. "I don't know about this. How do you want me to help you?"

"My nanobytes allow me to control the mind of any living thing that looks at my teeth. I want you to build a device that will allow me to do the same thing to computers. Once I have people and technology under my control, I will have the tools to destroy my enemies and rule the world." Simon laughed hysterically and his squirrels joined him.

"Wait, I thought you just wanted to destroy this one kid," Albert said. "You didn't tell me you wanted to take over the world."

Simon's eyes shone in the spotlight. "Albert, I'm an evil genius. It's always about taking over the world. Oh, don't frown. I think it's a small price to pay for superpowers, don't you?"

38°53 N, 77°05 W

Like a lot of gym teachers, Coach Babcock loved to torture his students. He felt he had failed as a teacher if his students didn't cry out for mercy. He often bragged that he held the school district's record for causing the most hysterical breakdowns in one afternoon. He used such classic forms of torture as weight training, wrestling, long-distance running, rope climbing, wind sprints, chin-ups, and the occasional game of wet dodgeball (the wet ball was superloud when it hit a kid, and it left a huge red welt). But his favorite device of torment was so horrible, so truly evil, that it would drive most children to the brink of madness. It was the square dance.

For six weeks of the school year, his students suffered through the Star Promenade, the Slip the Clutch, and the Ferris Wheel. As Babcock saw it, square dancing was the most embarrassing and uncomfortable form of dancing ever created, and a perfect way to prepare his students for the crushing heartbreak of life. Square dancing was a metaphor for life—you got swung around and just when you thought you were free, you got dragged back into the dance. He really thought he was doing the kids a favor.

But he couldn't teach them if the tornado alarm kept going off in the middle of a do-si-do, like it was now. Babcock looked out the window at the crystal-blue sky and sighed. Arlington had more tornado warnings than any place he had ever lived, and all of them were false alarms. He considered ignoring the siren and forcing his class to continue to Flip the Diamond, but if a tornado came after all and one of the kids got blown away, well, he'd be in for *another* disciplinary hearing. Discouraged, he ordered the children out through the double doors to the basement, where they would be safe. He left the gym empty, except for the sounds of fiddles and banjos coming from the old record player.

When everyone was gone, a slender hand removed the needle from the dusty record and the music stopped. Ms. Lisa Holiday locked the double doors that led out of the gym, then did the same to the emergency door. When she was satisfied there were no prying eyes, she rushed across the recently waxed gym floor, her high heels tapping out every step. When she got to the thick rope that hung down from the rafters, she grasped it in both hands and gave it three quick tugs. At once an unseen machine began to rumble beneath her feet. A blue light on the gym wall started to flash and the ceiling above slowly and silently retracted, revealing the bright blue sky above.

"All clear," she said, and a wall of the gym spun around and a team of scientists in white coats rushed into the room, followed by a team of mechanics wearing bright orange jumpsuits and hoods. Then part of the floor opened and slowly an enormous space jet rose up from below. It was painted yellow just like a school bus and had two huge wings and a needle nose. The mechanics busied themselves attaching huge fuel tubes to it while the scientists opened control panels and tinkered with its engine.

Finally, Agent Brand hobbled into the room with the help of his cane. Behind him were Duncan, Ruby, Matilda, Jackson, and Flinch.

Duncan smiled. He loved the School Bus—the name they had given the ship. He had seen plenty of spy movies with dashing heroes, but none of them had a space jet! He rushed to it and was soon climbing up the side like a spider. He startled a scientist standing on a lift checking the wind calculators in the ship's nose. The man tumbled backward. Luckily, Matilda was already zipping about using her superinhalers and managed to snatch him in free fall. She dropped him into Flinch's strong arms.

"Sorry," Duncan called out sheepishly.

The scientist was not amused. He shouted at the boy angrily and stormed off to file an official complaint.

Jackson's braces sprang out of his mouth and lifted him up to where Duncan was perched.

"Don't worry about it," Jackson said. "I've got a folder as thick as a phone book full of complaints. What can they do to us?"

"They can deduct fines from your pay," Ruby said from below.

"Hey! They pay us?" Jackson cried.

"Children, the lunch lady has been summoned and we'll be lifting off momentarily," Ms. Holiday said from below. "I need to prepare you for the mission. Come back down."

Duncan scurried down the side of the space jet and Jackson lowered himself to the floor, where they were joined by their teammates.

"Where are we going?" Ruby said.

"Edinburgh, Scotland," Agent Brand said. "Our friend Simon has resumed his criminal mischief. We've gotten word that he's trying to rob the Royal Bank of Scotland, but naturally, you five are going to stop him."

"Yes we are," Ruby said with confidence.

"And then I'm going to bodyslam him," Matilda said.

"Let's get this bird in the air," the lunch lady said as he ran through the open tunnel into the gym. "I've got a whole room of hungry kindergartners and you have no idea how vicious they can get when they have to wait on pizza day." He raced up the space jet's platform and leaped into the cockpit. A second later there was a rumbling roar and the engines ignited with blue flame.

Ms. Holiday and Mr. Brand led the children onto the ship and helped strap them into their seats. Within moments the space jet was blasting toward the stratosphere, leaving the gymnasium behind. Soon it was just a tiny spec outside the window.

"What do you think of our new School Bus?" Ms. Holiday asked Duncan.

Duncan smiled. The old rocket had been lost when the team was trying to stop Dr. Jigsaw from destroying the world. The new ship was ten times as fast. Unlike a plane, the School Bus didn't fly across the horizon as it went from point A to point B. Instead, it soared right up into space, waited for the planet to spin, then rocketed back down to the desired location. The method allowed them to travel anywhere on the planet in no time. It was how they managed to go on missions during school hours.

"It's an incredible machine and very efficient," Duncan said to Ms. Holiday. "The numbers I've read on fuel consumption are truly breathtaking. This machine gets gas mileage as good as a compact car."

"I like the snacks!" Flinch said as he opened four packages of caramels stored beneath his seat.

Duncan shrugged. He couldn't expect his teammate to get as excited about technology as he did. Most of the team had little interest in understanding the tools they had at their disposal as long as the tools worked. Ruby knew her way around computers, but her fancy pocket notebook with its state-of-the-art processor was just a laptop computer to her. Duncan, however, saw machines, no matter how small or simple, as miracles. He marveled at the imagination required to design them. So much love and passion had gone into them—sparked by a flash of genius. Machines were truly dreams come to life.

His teammates would have been surprised to discover that Duncan hadn't always had a love of learning and technology. In fact, just a few years before, he had been a below-average student, in a below-average school, in a below-average neighborhood. As a third grader at Elmhurst Elementary, a school notorious for its discipline problems and filled with exhausted teachers, he drifted down hallways like a ghost. He was shy and had few friends. And because his parents had taught him to respect teachers, the few friends he did have thought he was weird. He was in serious jeopardy of falling through the cracks—until the day he became a school celebrity. It all happened by accident during one of Ms. Corron's art classes. That day, as Duncan worked furiously on a dried corn and peas paste portrait of his mother, he spotted Renee Seal sniffing a glob of dried craft glue she had found on her desk. Her neighbor, a notorious prankster named Kevin Houser, told her to eat it. When she refused, he resorted to the best means of coercion a third grader has at his disposal: He dared her.

The class held its collective breath, knowing the full nature of a dare. If Renee refused, she would be shamed by her peers—possibly even shunned. But a second sniff of the glob told Renee it was better to be friendless than eat paste. She declined. Kevin was triumphant and searched the class for another victim.

"What about you, Duncan? Are you brave enough to eat the glue?"

Duncan shook his head. He was busy trying to get a pea just right so that his mom didn't look like a Cyclops.

"I double dare you," Kevin said, causing every kid in the class to drop their project. A double dare was high stakes. For some, the tension of the moment would cause nightmares and bed-wetting.

Duncan eyed the glue, then scanned the classroom. Even Ms. Corron was sitting on the edge of her seat biting her fingernails. He had never gotten so much attention in his life. Every eye was on him. If he chickened out, he would be subjected to even more ridicule than usual. He had to do it. He had to be brave. He shrugged, snatched the glob off the desk, popped it into his mouth, chewed it, and swallowed to a symphony of "Ewwwww!"

"I can't believe you did it," Kevin said, looking stunned. "I bet you won't do it again."

"What's in it for me?" Duncan said.

"Five bucks," Kevin replied.

Duncan reached over and snatched the bottle off the table. He unscrewed the cap and poured it into his mouth. Then he licked his chops. "Pay up!"

Another giant "Ewwwwwwww!" rose up in the room. Ms. Corron nearly fainted.

Kevin reached into his pocket and handed Duncan a crumpled five-dollar bill. He didn't look angry at losing his money or even humiliated; in fact, he looked like he had just won the lottery. From that moment on, Kevin stuck to Duncan, well . . . like glue. He paraded the chubby boy through the school, boasting about his strange taste in food, turning Duncan into his own personal sideshow and offering to repeat the art class incident for anyone who was willing to pay to see it. Much to Duncan's surprise, lots of people were willing. He and Kevin did six shows a day, in empty broom closets, bathrooms, and the boiler room. There were even Saturday and Sunday matinees on the playground.

"Come see the amazing Gluestick—the boy who eats paste!"

Kevin took an unusually high cut of the money, 75 percent, but Duncan didn't mind. He was a star, getting more attention than he ever dreamed possible. Plus, he actually liked eating paste. It was soft, like custard, but with a woody flavor. Kevin said it would ruin the show if the kids suspected that eating paste was a pleasant thing to do. He didn't want a copycat act muscling in on their spotlight. So Duncan pretended to loathe it.

Soon, however, Duncan and Kevin's carnival act came to the attention of the principal, who brought it to the attention of Avery and Aiah. Duncan's parents listened to details of the whole tawdry scheme while staring at their son as if he had six heads. The next day, his parents started looking for a home in a new school district far away from Elmhurst Elementary and Kevin Houser.

Nathan Hale Elementary was one of the best public schools in the state, and it was nestled in a tree-lined community that offered the family a fresh start. The mortgage was crippling, but if Duncan's parents saved and scrimped and cut coupons, the family would survive. The struggle would be worth it to get their kid back on the right track. Unfortunately, what Avery and Aiah didn't know was that Kevin Houser had a cousin at Nathan Hale by the name of Brett Bealer. Kevin had told Brett all about Duncan's taste for sticky adhesives, but unlike his more business-minded relative, Brett used the information to taunt Duncan, not profit from him. Before the boy could make a single friend, he was awarded a series of mean nicknames: Paste Boy, Sticky, Elmerface, Crazyglue. The list went on and on. It looked as if someone had flipped the Off switch on Duncan's bright new start.

That was until a young boy with the biggest set of buckteeth he had ever seen approached Duncan in the cafeteria.

"Are you the kid who eats the paste?"

Duncan nodded, his face bright red with embarrassment.

"My name is Heathcliff Hodges. I represent a group of people who would like to meet you. We believe you have the makings of a hero."

Now, Heathcliff's face haunted Duncan's memory. The boy with the big teeth had recruited him onto the team and helped train him. Duncan had been more surprised and saddened than anyone when Heathcliff betrayed them. He didn't like the idea of having to face his former friend again.

"How do we know Heathcliff is robbing this bank?" Jackson asked now.

"Police reports are claiming that dozens of squirrels are scampering around inside. There was also a trail of walnut shells on the sidewalk," Agent Brand replied.

"BEAEEAGGGCH," Flinch cried, then turned the knob on his harness. The caramels had sent him into an overexcited fit. "Sounds like our nutcase. Don't worry, we'll handle him. And this time we'll make sure we catch him."

"Ms. Holiday, a little information about our destination, please," Brand said.

Ms. Holiday stood up, straightened her skirt, then waved her hand over a sensor. Behind her a map of Scotland appeared on a bank of monitors.

"Scotland is part of the United Kingdom. It consists of over 790 islands and has an ancient culture dating back to the Neolithic period."

"Um, the what period?" Jackson asked.

"The stone ages," Ruby snarled. "Don't you ever do your homework?"

"My strategy is to coast on my looks," Jackson said, then stuck his tongue out at her.

Ms. Holiday continued. "Much of the country's history is that of internal wars and those with its southern neighbor, England. The population has strong nationalist pride, and it's not uncommon to see men wearing the traditional Scottish garb known as the kilt."

The computer screen showed a man carrying a briefcase and wearing a skirt.

"The modern Scot wears the kilt as a sign of national pride and as part of formal business attire. If you encounter someone wearing one, show them respect. It takes a tough man to wear a skirt in the frosty Scottish air."

"That means no giggling," Ruby said, eyeballing Jackson.

"Holiday is right, kids," the lunch lady said from his cockpit. "My father was Scottish, and the last thing you wanted to do was make fun of his kilt."

"You're headed to the Bank of Scotland on Picardy Place, not far from Princes Street, in the capital of Edinburgh. The bank is one of Europe's oldest, dating back to the seventeenth century," the librarian added. "You can imagine that a company that's been around since the seventeenth century has learned a thing or two about security. Their system is one of the most advanced in the world. Motion and heat sensors; twenty-four-hour surveillance; a vault that will drop into a thirty-story pit if it is accessed without permission."

"It was featured in last month's *Security Systems Magazine*. Everything is state-of-the-art," Duncan said.

"Only you would read something called *Security Systems Magazine*," Matilda said, grinning at Duncan.

He shrugged. "What I'm saying is it would take a genius to rob it."

"Unfortunately, Choppers is a genius," Agent Brand said gruffly. "You're going to have to be smarter than he is."

"Does anyone else feel like all of this doesn't add up?" Ruby said.

"Do you have concerns, Pufferfish?" Brand asked.

"As you know, I'm allergic to fish. I'm also allergic to things that feel fishy. My feet are swollen and my throat is scratchy, so I know something is not right. Why would Simon try to rob the world's most robbery-proof bank, in the heart of an international city, on a busy street, when he knows we are watching him?"

Duncan said, "I have been wondering the same thing."

Brand shook his head. "I don't like this. I don't like it at all. Simon . . . Heathcliff . . . Choppers—whatever his name is—he's unpredictable and dangerous. If I could send some more seasoned agents—"

"More seasoned agents?" Ruby cried. The rest of the team grumbled their protest.

"Enough!" Brand shouted. "All I'm saying is this boy used to be your friend and he may try to use that to his advantage.

But remember, he is not your friend anymore. I think last year's events prove he shouldn't be taken lightly. When you get inside the bank, keep your eyes open for a trap. Keep an eye on your partners, too. I can't lose another one of you."

"We're over the drop," the lunch lady shouted from the cockpit. "If you're near a butcher, pick me up some haggis. I think the students will love it."

Ms. Holiday opened a compartment and removed five different colored jackets. She gave one to each of them.

"What's this?" Jackson asked.

"These are the LX-919 Wind Breakers. They're the latest in parachute technology. Unlike a regular parachute, the Wind Breaker doesn't require careful packing. Once you hit two thousand feet, the jacket expands to capture the air below you. You'll float like a feather and there's no tracking down the parachute and storing it once you've landed. It collapses back into a jacket on the ground."

Duncan's eyes grew big with wonder. "Wow!"

Flinch laughed. "Gluestick loves his gadgets."

"The Wind Breaker will also keep you warm in high altitudes. The wind can be pretty brisk off those Highlands," Ms. Holiday said to the children. "I don't want my sweethearts to freeze."

"Sweethearts?" Matilda muttered.

Ms. Holiday blushed. The librarian had a motherly quality with the children she could barely control. "I mean 'agents.'"

Flinch grinned and winked at her. "I'll be your sweetheart."

Jackson slid into his Wind Breaker. "Are you sure about this thing? I have a problem with falling to my death. It's not in my job description."

"These are better than any parachutes," Ms. Holiday assured him. "Once you get to a thousand feet above the ground, just pull the strings at the bottom of the jacket and you will activate the air-to-ground tether."

"'Air-to-ground tether' does not sound better to me than 'nice, big parachute,'" Jackson argued.

"C'mon, Braceface, parachutes are so last week," Duncan said as he clapped his hands. He couldn't wait to give the new gadget a try.

While the children put on their gear, Agent Brand popped open the hatch and wind blasted into the ship.

"Pufferfish, as always, you lead this mission," Brand shouted over the din. "Keep an eye on all movement from the roof of the bank and use the rest of the team's abilities to find and arrest Heathcliff. Be careful! The rest of you, look out for one another!"

"As good as done, sir," Ruby said.

"Any words of encouragement for our heroes, Mr. Brand?" Ms. Holiday asked.

Brand frowned. Duncan knew the man wasn't the type to give pep talks or sappy speeches. He hardly talked at all, despite Ms. Holiday's constant efforts to get him to warm to the children.

He grunted and scowled and finally said, "Don't get killed."

"Well, I'm inspired," Matilda said. Then she leaped out of the door into the wide blue sky. Flinch was next, shouting, "Cannonball!" as he went. Ruby took her turn, followed by Jackson, who used his last moments on board to plead with Ms. Holiday for a real parachute. Duncan was last.

"Gluestick, I know Heathcliff and you were close," Brand said. "But use your head. He's the enemy now."

"Of course, sir," Duncan replied, pushing any concern from his mind. "I know my job. We'll stop him."

He leaped out into the sky, feeling the wind swim around his body. Gravity pulled him downward, faster and faster. He could see his teammates far below—tiny black specks dropping like rain. Suddenly, he heard a ping inside his head, followed by Ruby's voice. She had activated the communications system implanted in each of their noses, the one that made them sneeze when they were summoned to the Playground. "Here's the plan, people—Wheezer and Braceface, you are on crowd control inside the bank. The police believe there may be anywhere from ninety to a hundred people inside. Please be careful. Try to use your abilities as little as possible in front of hostages. It's hard to be a secret agent if the secret is out. Flinch, you're going to get us inside."

"How?" Flinch's voice said.

"You are going to karate chop the building."

"Awesome sauce!" he cried. "I'll start eating some candy now to power up."

"Gluestick, you're our fly on the wall. I want you crawling on the ceiling, staying out of sight and looking for our target. You know standard protocol. If you spot Simon, don't engage him until one of us can help. I'll be on the roof, scanning the building and feeding all of you information. As always, stay in constant contact with one another."

"Um, I'm a little worried about my Wind Breaker," Jackson said. "It looked like a jacket and so far it's acting like one too."

"Keep your mouth shut, quarterback, or you'll miss it," Matilda replied.

"Miss what?"

"The moment we break the sound barrier." Matilda giggled. There was a tremendous sonic boom in the sky and suddenly the ground was flying toward them at an amazing speed. Duncan's Wind Breaker expanded, catching the air inside and slowing his descent as if he were a dandelion seed floating in the wind.

"These things are pretty neat, huh?" Duncan said.

"Yeah, real neat. I think I lost my lunch twenty thousand feet ago," Jackson groaned.

"I liked it better when we were going faster," Flinch cheered. He reached into his pocket and took out a bottle of energy drink. He guzzled it, then looked at the can as if he might eat it.

"We're approaching a thousand feet," Ruby chimed in. "Prepare to pull your tether chords."

"Nineteen hundred," Matilda said.

"Eighteen hundred," Duncan replied. "It would be best if we linked arms."

The children had all had skydiving training and had performed hundreds of tandem and single jumps. They knew how to maneuver in the sky, so with a few simple body adjustments they formed a circle and linked arms.

"Now try to point your feet toward the ground," Duncan instructed.

"Seventeen hundred feet," Jackson said.

Duncan looked below. He could see a busy commercial district and a series of intertwining roads weaving like worms in all directions.

"Sixteen hundred feet," said Matilda.

"Get ready, people," Ruby ordered.

38°53 N, 77°05 W

"Um, what if these don't work?" Jackson said.

"Then we go splat!" Flinch cried, breaking into a giggle.

"Fifteen hundred feet . . . fourteen hundred feet . . . thirteen hundred feet . . . twelve hundred feet . . . eleven hundred feet . . . OK, folks, let's activate the tethers," cried Ruby.

The children reached down and yanked on the cords around the bottoms of their jackets. Duncan immediately felt something rocket out of his jacket. When he looked down he saw it was a cable that spiraled to the top of a building directly beneath them. It slammed into the roof like an arrow and suddenly the cable stiffened into something as hard as a fireman's pole. Duncan snatched the cable, sliding down it until his feet were on the top of the Royal Bank of Scotland. His Wind Breaker returned to its jacket form and the cable slackened back into a rope.

Flinch was the second to land on the bank. Jackson was next. Then Ruby. Matilda took a bad landing and nearly skidded off the top of the roof, but Duncan snatched her by the arm and held her fast.

"Thanks, I owe you," Matilda said as her jacket retracted.

"Not a problem," Duncan said.

Ruby set up her laptop. The screen came to life. "OK, I'm linked in and pulling up the schematics of the bank. Looks as if there are three levels. The second floor is mostly offices, the ground floor is where the tellers are, and the basement is a deep shaft going down thirty feet. Gluestick was right. If you mess with that vault, you better have a shovel. Satellite heat scans are showing that the customers are lying on the floor and there is a figure moving about the bank."

"How do we get in?" Jackson asked as he pulled off his Wind Breaker.

"That's the spaz's job," Ruby said, gesturing to Flinch.

Flinch grinned and shoved three chocolate bars into his mouth at once. He chewed greedily and swallowed. Duncan watched as a blue light shone out of Flinch's harness. His hyperactivity was fueling it—making him superstrong. "I am mighty!" the boy roared, beating on his chest.

"He's ready," Jackson said.

Flinch leaned down and karate chopped the rooftop with his bare hand. There was a crack and a giant chunk of the roof fell inward, sending up a cloud of dust and debris.

"Subtle," Matilda said.

Ruby cocked an eyebrow. "Get in there, Wheezer."

Matilda fired her inhalers and zipped straight up into the air. When she turned them off, she dropped like a rock into the hole. Duncan watched her fire them up at the last second so she hovered safely just above the floor. Flinch leaped in too, landing on his feet as nimbly as a cat.

"Looks like I'm next," Jackson said as his obnoxious braces swirled inside his mouth. Soon, a huge, spindly pair of legs made from his dental gear came out of his mouth and lowered him inside.

"All right, Gluestick, you're up. Search the rooms and report back what you see. Once you've found Heathcliff, I'll send the others to find you. No heroics, OK? I want to take him as a team."

Duncan kicked off his shoes and got onto his hands and knees. He crawled into the hole. With his sticky toes and fingertips, he felt for the ceiling, then clung to it as he scuttled inside the bank. He raced across the ceiling, moving cautiously from doorway to doorway down the long corridor. After a few minutes of searching, he reported back to Ruby, "There's no one on the second floor."

Ruby's voice was in his ears. "Good. Move down to the first floor."

Duncan tiptoed down a flight of stairs, then ran up a wall until he was once again upside-down. He came to an open door that led to the bank lobby and crawled inside. He saw the customers Ruby had warned him about. A hundred or so people were lying facedown, their hands on their heads. Some were quietly crying and a few looked as if they might be sick. A beefy guard in a green kilt was handcuffed to a heavy desk and couldn't move. But what was most troubling to Duncan wasn't the hostages. It was the squirrels. A dozen or so stood over the cowering people like tiny rodent sentries. A few more were dragging bags of money toward the bank entrance and stacking them by the door. More were rifling through wallets and stealing jewelry right off the fingers of the terrified victims. Duncan had seen a lot of strange things in his life, especially since becoming a spy, but this was the strangest.

"Gluestick, report please," Ruby's voice demanded.

"I've got squirrels," he whispered. "They're all over the place."

"Yes, Brand mentioned them. How many of them are there?"

"Maybe thirty. Maybe more."

"Any sign of Simon?" Ruby asked.

Duncan glanced around the room. "No, he's not in the main room. There are some small offices off to the—wait, I hear shouting. Hang on."

Duncan followed the noise and soon found the manager's office. A plump woman in a smart suit was cowering on the floor. She had bright red hair and freckles.

"Do what ye want but ye willnae get into the vault," she cried in her thick Scottish accent. "Even if I gave ye the codes, ye need two other managers to open the door and they are currently on holiday. Just take what ye have and go."

Duncan could not see Simon, but he could see what looked like a ray gun from a science fiction movie pointed at the manager.

"Simon's got some kind of weapon aimed at the manager," Duncan whispered. "I'm not close enough to guess what it does. Can you scan it?"

"I can see it, but whatever it is, it seems to be jamming the satellites," Ruby said. "Stay put. The bank manager is in danger. I'm sending for the team."

"I don't need you to give me the codes," a voice said from within the room. Duncan was startled. What he heard was not Simon's voice. In fact, it sounded like the voice of a full-grown man. "The computer will give them to me."

The mysterious unseen man pointed his weapon at the manager's computer and pulled the trigger. At once the screen went berserk. Numbers and letters did a nervous dance across the monitor. The machine chirped and beeped and then Duncan could see the door to the vault slowly open.

"How did ye do that?" the manager cried.

"That would be telling. Squirrels!" the man shouted, and before Duncan could react, a sea of furry criminals raced into the room. He watched as they zipped into the vault with their sacks, filling them to the brim with cash, bonds, and jewelry, and then dragged their loot back into the main room with the rest.

"Pufferfish, whoever this is, it isn't Heathcliff. It's some old dude and he's fired his weapon," Duncan whispered. "It seems to be affecting the computer. He's got the door of the vault open now."

He didn't get a response. All he could hear was an odd static sound. "Please advise. Pufferfish, are you there? Pufferfish, come in." Still there was no answer. Duncan decided to move closer. Suddenly, he felt very ill. His stomach churned and his face felt hot. His hands and feet were itchy, and before he knew what had happened, his fingers and toes lost their grip on the ceiling. He fell to the floor, where he lay at the feet of a strange, overweight man in a black-and-green outfit.

"The boss warned me about you," the man said nervously. Duncan had never met a villain with such lack of confidence. "I guess if you're here then the others are on their way. Squirrels, get what you can. We have to go!"

"Who are you?" Duncan asked as he tried to stand. He could make out red eyebrows and a freckled face behind the mask, but not much else.

"Captain Just—you know what, it doesn't matter who I am," the man said.

He shooed his furry cohorts out the door and followed them, keeping his ray gun aimed at Duncan the whole time. Duncan wanted to glue the man to the wall behind him, but he couldn't seem to activate the adhesives on his hands properly. The ability would work for a moment and then it would vanish just as quickly.

"Step into the vault, kid," the man said.

Helpless, Duncan did as he was told. He had no idea what the weapon could do, but he was smart enough not to want to find out. Once Duncan was inside, the man leveled his weird ray gun at the boy's chest. There was a flash of light and Gluestick felt as if he were no longer in control of his body. His feet and hands were producing the sticky film that allowed him to walk on walls at an alarming rate. It was literally pouring out of him like a garden hose, circling his feet and locking him to the floor. Within seconds he couldn't move. He was like a mouse in a glue trap.

"Sorry, kid," the man said, then fired his weapon at the vault itself. Duncan watched helplessly as the door closed tight, and then, with a sudden jerk, the vault plunged downward. The villain had triggered the security system. Duncan was stuck tight inside a vault that had just plummeted thirty feet below the ground.

6

55°57 N, 03°11 W

"Do you like what you see, boss?" Albert's voice said.

Simon was watching the action on a laptop computer in a tiny Internet café on Princes Street. The place was filled with losers writing stage plays and epic novels. Worse, the customers kept staring at him in his cloak and mask. Hadn't they ever seen an evil mastermind before? He shrugged them off. He wouldn't let them ruin his good time. Albert's invention worked! With one zap, computers, machines, anything with an electronic intelligence, had been bent to his will. Best of all, it hypnotized the nanobytes inside Simon's former friend, Duncan, disabling him.

"Most impressive," Simon said, "but where are the . . ." Just then he heard Flinch's war cry over the monitor. "Look out, Albert!" he cried to the man on the screen. But it was too late. Simon watched as his hyperactive former teammate ran toward

Albert at top speed, turning into a colorful blur before coming to a sudden stop. Flinch grabbed the man by one of his huge legs and lifted him off the ground like he was a marshmallow.

"I caught a bad guy! I caught a bad guy!" Flinch sang.

"Put me down," Albert demanded, but when Flinch refused, he aimed his ray gun at the boy and fired. Flinch immediately dropped his prize and stared at his own hands in disbelief. Then, suddenly, the boy started running out of control until he slammed into a wall, face-first. He fell down, unconscious.

"What did you do to him?" a familiar voice yelled. Simon peered into the computer screen to see Matilda racing forward.

"You kids just stay back," Albert stuttered. For a guy who wanted to be a superhero, he certainly didn't have a lot of confidence. "Stay back!"

Matilda fired her inhalers and flew at him, kicking Albert in the head. The roly-poly man stumbled backward, struggling with his mask, which had slid down over his eyes. While he was disabled, Matilda went in for another attack, but Albert managed to fix his mask just in time to fire his weapon at her too. She fell to the floor with a painful thud.

Jackson and Ruby were next, and didn't fare much better. As soon as they attacked, Albert shot them with the ray gun, as well.

When all four kids lay on the ground at Albert's feet, Simon

heard Ruby hiss, "So, are you another one of Heathcliff's lackeys?"

Albert was confused. "I don't know a Heathcliff. I work for Simon."

"Oh, they're the same guy. We also used to call him Choppers. He was one of us until he betrayed us and tried to destroy the world. Did he mention that to you?"

"I don't need to know anything about him."

"Well, you should know one thing, buddy. Your boss is a whiny crybaby filled with bitterness because he was never cool. It's a fatal flaw and we will always beat him because of it. Unfortunately, you're never going to get to tell him because you're going to jail."

"Whiny crybaby!" Simon cried. Everyone in the café stared at him but he didn't care. "I will destroy you all! I will crush you into pulp and you will beg me for mercy but there will be none. Simon will have his revenge!"

"You ready for another root beer, kid?" the waitress asked.

Simon spun in his chair and gave her an angry look. "If you have any hope of a tip, I suggest you leave me alone. Can't you see I'm busy?"

"Fine," the waitress grumbled and shuffled off to another customer. Simon turned back to the café's computer and typed furiously. The "C" and backslash keys kept sticking, victims of too many spilled chai lattes. Still, what he had seen on the video had set his mind afire with inspiration. He would use Albert's schematics to build a weapon big enough to knock out the world's machines and put the human race in his control. And it looked as if there was nothing Gluestick, Wheezer, Braceface, Flinch, or Pufferfish could do about it. The other upside was that he would soon have enough money to move his base of operations to a proper secret lair where he wasn't competing with birds, chipmunks, raccoons, and cats for space, and the rest of the evil villain community would stop laughing at him.

Now, with the money he was swiping from banks, he could build a new, glorious secret headquarters from which to devise evil plans. He typed furiously at the keyboard, making notes on his evil master bathroom, the evil solarium where he would devise evil plots, and the evil meeting room with the long, evil oak table where he would intimidate his evil underlings. But nothing made him smile like the evil mirrored room where he would taunt his enemies, causing them to believe there were thousands of him. He had seen that in a movie and it was supercool.

"The first thing I'm going to build in my new secret lair is an Internet café where I am the only customer," he said loudly enough for the other customers to hear. "I will have robot waitresses who are not so incompetent and absolutely no one working on a blog."

SUPPLEMENTAL EVIDENCE

The following are intercepted
e-mails sent from Simon to Steven
Ostwick, a Bethesda-based licensed
contractor and architect.

From: simon@simonsaysobeyme.com
Date: March 20
To: Steven Ostwick
Subject: My Secret Lair

Steven,

Great to talk to you on the phone, and I'm very excited to get started on my secret lair. As I said, I have big ideas for this project and I'm glad you are excited as well. I'm attaching a rough drawing I did myself of what the lair should look like (of course, I'm open to your ideas as well, but I must, must, must have my shark tank. lol). Please let me know you got this and feel free to contact me with any questions you might have.

ttyl,

Your master,

Simon

From: Steven Ostwick
Date: March 21
To: simon@simonsaysobeyme.com
Subject: RE: My Secret Lair

Dear Simon,

Thank you for sending my retainer so promptly. I have taken a look at your designs and I have a few concerns. I must admit I have never designed and built a secret lair before. The closest I've come was a very fancy tree house for a billionaire's son. I have no experience with trapdoors, flaming pits, moats, dungeons, or giant industrial saws intended for "cutting your enemies in half." Most of my designs are small projects like bathroom remodeling or building outdoor structures like sheds. As long as you are aware of this, I will be happy to tackle these challenging ideas.

My biggest concern comes from the giant laser intended to protect your fortress from attacks by land and air. I've looked at your rough sketch and have to be very up-front with you. Something that big could overwhelm the structure. I fear it would weigh too much and jeopardize your foundation.

I also have a lot of questions about the room you call "the mutation lab."

Best,

Steven

Date: March 21

Subject: RE: RE: My Secret Lair

Dear Steve-O!

Got your e-mail. If something is wrong, I will tie you to a rocket and shoot you into space—lol. Do my bidding!

Fear me,

Simon

Date: March 21

Subject: RE: RE: RE: My Secret Lair

Hey Simon,

The guys and I laughed so hard about that rocket thing. You are one funny guy. Got some costs on the fire pits. I'll send them along.

Steven

Date: March 22

Subject: RE: RE: RE: RE: My Secret Lair

Steve-buddy,

No joke on the rocket. I will kill you. Did you get my ideas about the crown molding and the color samples?

Your worst nightmare,

Simon

Date: March 24

Subject: RE: RE: RE: RE: RE: My Secret Lair

Stevie,

Hey, did you get my last e-mail? Let me know how things are going.

The Dark Lord Simon

END TRANSMISSION.

OOOOHHHHH! WASN'T THAT
EXCITING? YOU KNOW, A LOT
OF KIDS READ THAT AND FREAK
OUT. I'M SERIOUS. THE LAST
TEN CANDIDATES HAD TO BE
TAKEN TO A MENTAL HOSPITAL
FOR SOME "RELAXATION."

ANYWAY, THE POWERS THAT BE
TOOK A LOOK AT YOUR CODE-
BREAKING SKILLS AND DECIDED
THAT IT WAS TIME TO TAKE
YOU TO THE NEXT LEVEL.
SO I'M GOING TO TEACH YOU
ABOUT SOMETHING CALLED A
SUBSTITUTION CIPHER WHEEL.
THIS IS A CODE METHOD THAT
GOES ALL THE WAY BACK TO THE
TIME OF JULIUS CAESAR, WHO,
WITH HIS TOGA, SANDALS,
AND LEAF HEADBAND, WAS
A TOTAL B.C. NERD.

HERE'S HOW IT WORKS: YOU HAVE
TWO CIRCLES MADE FROM THE
LETTERS OF THE ALPHABET.
A BIG ONE:

WXYZABCDEFGHIJKLMNOPQRSTUV

AND A LITTLE ONE:

WXYZABCDEFGHIJKLMNOPQRSTUV

PHOTOCOPY THE CIRCLES
AND CUT OUT YOUR COPY.
OR, BETTER YET, CUT THIS BOOK
UP NOW AND GO OUT AND BUY
ANOTHER ONE TO READ—THAT'S
EXCELLENT FOR SALES. UNLESS
IT'S A LIBRARY BOOK, IN
WHICH CASE YOU'RE DEAD!

ALL RIGHT. NOW PAY ATTENTION,
'CAUSE THIS IS WHERE IT GETS
TRICKY. YOU MAKE COPIES OF THE
CIRCLES AND THEN CUT THEM OUT.
TAKE THE LITTLE CIRCLE AND PUT
IT ON TOP OF THE BIG CIRCLE
SO THAT ONE IS INSIDE THE
OTHER. GOT IT? GOOD.

NOW YOU CHOOSE A "KEY LETTER"
FOR THE SMALLER CIRCLE. THIS
LETTER WOULD BE SOMETHING ONLY
YOU AND THE RECIPIENT OF YOUR
MESSAGE WOULD KNOW. IF YOU HAVE
A KEY LETTER, LINE IT UP WITH
THE "A" ON THE BIG CIRCLE.

THE LETTERS ON THE BIG CIRCLE ARE THE ACTUAL ALPHABET AND THE ONES ON THE INNER CIRCLE ARE YOUR CODE ALPHABET. SELECT THE CODE LETTERS THAT LINE UP WITH THE LETTERS OF YOUR SECRET MESSAGE AND WRITE THEM DOWN.

HERE, LET'S TRY. I'M ASSIGNING THE LETTER "M" AS MY KEY LETTER. SEE IF YOU CAN DECIPHER MY SUPERSECRET MESSAGE.

EQDUAGEXK, PA EAYQFTUZS MNAGF KAGD RQQF.
FTQK EYQXX XUWQ M OAYNUZMFUAZ AR QSSE MZP
RMDFE. KAG'DQ XGOWK FA TMHQ M RDUQZP XUWQ
YQ ITA IUXX FQXX KAG ITQZ KAG'DQ RGZWK.

SORRY, BUT YOU CLEARLY
AREN'T GETTING THE MESSAGE.

LEVEL 3

ACCESS GRANTED

BEGIN TRANSMISSION:

7

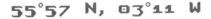
Duncan heard something crack-ing above him and watched as the metal ceiling turned from black to red to white-hot. He quickly realized that someone was using a blowtorch to cut through the vault—probably Matilda and her enhanced inhalers. He wished he could free himself from his own glue, but all he could do was watch. It was all very embarrassing.

Finally, a portion of the roof fell to the ground and Agent Brand poked his head inside. He stared at Duncan for a moment and frowned. The man's disappointment felt like a punch in the belly.

"We'll get you out of here soon, son," Brand said.

Duncan quietly wondered if it wouldn't have been better to be trapped underground forever.

"Gluestick, did you hear me?" Ms. Holiday said. She and Agent Brand were watching him through a glass window in an adjacent room back at the Playground as a bank of green lights danced across his body. "Scans are showing that every nanobyte in your body has been infected with a computer virus that is destroying them one by one. Two-thirds of them are already off-line and the rest will be gone within the hour."

"Which means what exactly?" Duncan said.

"You're powerless," Benjamin said as the tiny orb hovered about the boy's face. "At least for the time being. You see, the nanobytes that give you your abilities are nothing more than microscopic computers. In your case, they produce the adhesive in your skin that makes you sticky. The ray gun that was fired at you basically rewrote their code, causing many of them to burn themselves out. The rest are acting most peculiar—like they are obeying completely different instructions."

"I know how the nanobytes work," Duncan said. He could feel a panic rising inside of him. "What are we going to do about it?"

"Gluestick, you and the rest of the team will have to have the nanobytes extracted and then we can put you through the upgrade process once more."

Duncan sighed. "I shouldn't have just barged in when I had no idea what or who was waiting for me."

"Duncan, you're being too hard on yourself," Ms. Holiday said. "You were concerned for the bank manager and—"

Agent Brand interrupted. "Actually, it was a major blunder."

Ms. Holiday bit her lip. "That is not helpful," she whispered.

"Gluestick has been trained by the best. He knows better than to race into the unknown," Brand said, standing his ground.

"How are the others?" Duncan asked. "Are they OK?"

"They've already gone through the scans and the results have been the same, Duncan," the librarian replied.

"You don't think Heathcliff's found some way to . . . you know, hypnotize machines the way he can people and animals, do you?" Duncan asked.

"It's our job to find out," Brand said. "When will the team be ready?"

"Three days," Benjamin said.

"Three days!" Brand cried. "Simon might control the world in three days!"

"I'm afraid I'm going to have to remove all of the nanobytes in each of the operatives."

"But Benjamin, we've taken the upgrades out of people before," Ms. Holiday said.

"Last year we took them out of Jackson and put them back in a couple days later," Duncan reminded them. "It didn't take three days for him to be back online."

"Jackson's nanobytes were receptive to my commands," Benjamin explained. "I asked them to leave and then asked them to return. The nanobytes in your body aren't listening. I'm going to have to hunt them down, one by one, until they are all collected. If I were to leave even one behind, it could infect the new ones. I can, however, reinstall the nasal implants that link the team with me."

Brand growled. "Get to work, Benjamin." He stormed out of the room, leaving Ms. Holiday alone to look in on Duncan.

"OK, well, don't worry, Gluestick," Ms. Holiday said. "Just relax and we'll have you back to fighting shape in no time."

It took all Duncan's strength to smile back. Inside he was feeling embarrassed, depressed, and foolish.

Duncan spent much of the day lying on a table inside the upgrade room having his nanobytes removed. He hadn't really noticed before, but he could feel them inside him. It was a subtle sensation, and not unpleasant, but as more and more of them were extracted, he felt more and more empty.

"While we are here, perhaps you would like to give me some information about your odd attacker," Benjamin said. "Perhaps we can put together a sketch from your details."

"Well, he was about five seven, maybe five eight, though his boots might have given him an inch or two."

Benjamin began to spin, and a million particles of light filled the room. Suddenly, there was a stick figure as tall as a man standing before him.

"Anything else?"

"He had kind of let himself go," Duncan said, pulling his T-shirt down over his own exposed belly. "He probably weighed three hundred pounds."

Suddenly the stick figure expanded into the shape of an obese man.

"Any facial features?"

"I didn't see much," Duncan said. "He was wearing a black mask that covered his face and hair. Oh, yeah. He had red eyebrows. He must be a redhead."

The stick figure grew red hair. Then a black mask was placed over its face, showing only the eyes.

"Eye color?"

"I don't know," Duncan said. "It happened so fast."

"We have some security footage, but we never got a shot of his face. Let me see if I can combine your description with what the cameras captured," Benjamin said. Suddenly, the round stick figure had hands and fingers. His costume was black and green, with a cape and a cursor symbol on the chest. Benjamin added boots and gloves and a belt buckle, but the face was not there.

"It's not a lot." Duncan sighed.

"Let me know if you remember anything else," the orb chirped. "I'll send this to Mr. Brand. As for your nanobytes, I think we're through for the day. Go home and get some rest."

Duncan exited through the lockers and walked down the school halls as students spilled out of classrooms, headed for their buses. He felt small and weak. When he was full of superpower, he had strolled along without a care. Sure, a school bully might confront him, but he had always taken this in stride. After all, he was an international spy. He traveled the world. He could stick to walls. His double life had always been the great equalizer. No matter how many wedgies he received, he could smile with the knowledge that he was special. Now he was average . . . again.

Flinch met him outside. They decided to skip the bus ride and walk home.

"This must be very hard on you," Duncan said to his friend. "Your upgrades not only give you abilities, they help control your hyperactivity."

Flinch looked visibly shaky. "Benjamin said that I should stay away from candy and soda until I'm back online. You have no idea how hard it is not to stuff my face with graham crackers right now."

"I'm sorry. It was my fault we got zapped," Duncan said.

"You're being crazy, D. You can't blame yourself because you were surprised. We all thought we'd find Simon, not some giant tub of a dude having a midlife crisis with a ray gun. You did exactly what I would have done. Plus, you bought us a three-day vacation. It'll give Jackson a chance to catch up on his reports."

"Three days of being regular," Duncan said. The thought gave him the jitters.

"I know how I can cheer you up," Flinch said. "You can invite me over for dinner. I am an amazing dinner guest and I know how much the Creature likes me."

Duncan wanted to laugh, but his dismal mood hung over him like a rain cloud.

Dinner at Duncan's house was always a noisy affair. His family enjoyed discussing their days, usually all at once. There was a genuine excitement about being together. Aiah told them about a family she was working with who was trying to get out of a homeless shelter. Avery talked and talked about the Aston Martin he had worked on that afternoon, and how exhilarating it was to take it for a test drive. "I felt like a spy," he said, smiling at his son. The Creature complained about teachers, boys, girls, her friends, her enemies, Duncan, her parents, and everyone else who crossed her path.

"And what about you two?" Aiah asked as she snatched the bag of peppermints out of Flinch's hand and put another scoop of lima beans on his plate. "I know you can't tell me everything, but did anything exciting happen today?"

Duncan and Flinch shared a look.

"Same old same old, Mrs. Dewey," Flinch said. "Just another boring day at school."

"Oh, I hate when you say that," Aiah sighed. "It always makes me think something dangerous happened and you just aren't allowed to talk about it."

"I'm sure they both got wedgied and shoved into lockers," the Creature said. "Same old story for members of the nerd herd."

"Be nice, Tanisha," Avery said.

"Relax, Dad," the Creature said. "Flinch and dumb-dumb here have superpowers. I'm sure they can handle my insults."

Duncan and Flinch shared another uncomfortable look.

After dinner, the boys insisted on loading the dishwasher. Duncan couldn't wait to get his hands on the remote control. Pressing its buttons gave him comfort after such a depressing day. He typed in a code and soon a robotic arm was snatching dirty dishes off the dining room table, rinsing them, and inserting them into the slots of the dishwasher. Then it closed the door and the machine started its cleaning cycle.

Avery watched the action from the kitchen table. He was scanning the classified section of the newspaper for auto parts. He had been restoring a 1968 Ford Mustang convertible since before Duncan was born. It took up most of the garage. Besides a paint job, it was nearly complete. Avery wanted every part to be from the original make, and they weren't easy to find. Some weekends he spent hours digging through the local junkyard for the finishing touches—rearview mirrors, factory hubcabs, and an original AM radio.

"You and your machines," he said now with a sigh. "You want to see a real machine, look out in the garage. The Mustang is a machine made with love and care. There's a heart to it."

"That's true, but can the Mustang do this?" Duncan asked as he pushed a few more buttons on his remote. Suddenly, the cabinets opened and a robotic hand opened the dishwasher and tossed the clean dishes into the air. They landed in the cabinets with perfect aim and without a chip. Everything was put away in a flash.

Avery rolled his eyes. "You kids are never going to understand. I can appreciate a fancy gadget. All I'm saying is, don't let all these gizmos make you lazy—both in the body and the mind." He snatched up his paper and headed off to the living room.

"He's not a big fan of the technology, huh?" Flinch said as he searched the freezer for some ice cream.

"I think he'd prefer it if we lived in a log cabin without any electricity," Duncan said. He handed Flinch a spoon and the boy went to work on a tub of orange sherbet he found behind a bag of peas. "Want to see if there are any bad guys up to no good?"

"Duh!"

The boys raced down the hallway to Duncan's room and closed the door tight behind them. Duncan reached into his pocket and took out Benjamin. The orb glowed bright blue, then floated out of his hand.

"What can I do for you, agents?"

"Activate Surveillance Room," Duncan said, and suddenly the bedroom furniture vanished and the supercomputer reappeared. TV monitors displayed images from around the globe.

"It's pretty cool that Brand lets you take one of the Benjamin orbs home with you," Flinch said.

"Actually, it was Ms. Holiday's idea. She's been encouraging me to spend my free time looking for trouble around the world. Plus, Benjamin is great at helping me with homework. So, Benjamin, any bad guys doing some bad stuff out there?"

"It appears you have one right outside," Benjamin said. "Look!"

Duncan looked at one of the monitors. It revealed a scene from right outside of his house. There, standing in the backyard by the garage, was a tall teenage boy, probably close to eighteen years old. He was leaning against the Deweys' garage door.

"Who's that?" Flinch asked.

Duncan shrugged but kept watching until a moment later he

spotted Tanisha sneaking out the back door. The boy leaned down and kissed her.

"Oh, I think I just threw up in my mouth a little," Flinch said. "Who in this world would want to kiss the Creature?"

"Maybe he's blind," Duncan said.

Then the teenager reached into his pocket and pulled out a pack of cigarettes. He passed one to Tanisha, who lit it and took some puffs. Duncan's jaw dropped open.

"What should we do? Tell your parents?" Flinch asked.

"No, we'll handle this," Duncan said.

"Are you forgetting how mean your sister can be? The Creature is like a rottweiler!"

Despite Flinch's concerns, he marched outside with Duncan. They found Tanisha and her friend in a tight embrace.

"Put out the cigarette," Duncan demanded.

"Oh, hey little man. No need to get so angry," Tanisha's boyfriend said. "I'm TJ."

Duncan ignored him. "Tanisha, put it out or I'm going to tell Dad."

"Who is this kid, Tanisha? Your own private bodyguard or something?"

"He's nobody and he's about to go back inside and mind his own business," Tanisha said, flashing Duncan an angry look.

"I mean it, Tanisha," Duncan said.

"Yo, little man," TJ said. "How about you go play some video games, and leave your sister and me alone?"

"OK, your call," Duncan said to his sister. "Daaaaaad!"

TJ leaped in front of Duncan. "Now that's not nice. Didn't your parents teach you about tattling, little man?"

"My name is Duncan and my parents taught me to look out for bad influences and ugly people. You happen to be both so you're easy to spot."

TJ grabbed him by the collar. "You better watch your mouth."

"TJ! Let him go," Tanisha demanded.

Flinch stepped up to the much bigger boy. "I'm giving you three seconds to let him go," he said. "After that I'm bringing the pain."

TJ laughed and snatched Flinch by the collar. He held the boys close to his face. "You getting smart with me too?"

Duncan knew exactly how to handle TJ. He wouldn't come around again if he spent two days glued to the roof. Duncan concentrated to activate his nanobytes then remembered—he was powerless!

"One," Flinch said.

"Flinch, leave him alone," Tanisha begged.

"Leave me alone?" TJ shouted. "Babe, I'm three times their size."

"Two."

"Now, let's get something straight. You're going back into the house and you're not going to say a word."

"Three."

In a flash, Flinch had kicked TJ in the shin. When the older boy dropped the two spies, Flinch grabbed his wrist, twisting his arm behind his back until the guy screamed. Flinch followed this with a punch to TJ's sternum, and when the older boy bent over to catch his breath, Flinch climbed on his back, wrapped his arms around his throat, and put pressure on his carotid artery. TJ struggled for a moment, like a fish washed up on the sand, then slid to the ground—sound asleep.

"Why didn't you help me?" Flinch asked Duncan.

"What was I going to do? My upgrades are offline," he said.

"So are mine!" Flinch complained. "We've both been trained in mixed martial arts, dude."

The Creature was even more incensed than Flinch. She tossed her cigarette on the ground and stomped over to Duncan. He could see her rage and tried to explain.

"This guy is a loser—"

"No! The only loser around here is you. I don't need your protection and I don't want it! Take your nanobutts and mind your own business."

"They're called nano*bytes*, Tanisha. I know you're angry, but please keep your voice down—"

"What would happen if I shouted it for everyone to hear? What would happen if I screamed that my nerdy little brother is actually a spy? Would they drag me away? Put me in prison?"

"Yes," Flinch said.

Tanisha hesitated, then said furiously, "You should be worried about yourself, Duncan. You might be some national hero, but around here you're a misfit."

"What do you mean 'around here'?"

"You're nothing like us, Duncan," she cried. "Who are you like? Dad? Mom? Me? You're a circus freak who shares our house—with your secret life and your stupid gizmos. Don't you see how Mom and Dad look at you? It's like you're from another planet. It's because of you we moved to this stupid neighborhood, too. Haven't you noticed that no one within a mile looks like us? Haven't you noticed that I don't have any friends here? It's all because *you* have to be different. *You* have to be special. The rest of us are fine just being us, but Duncan needs the whole world to notice him."

Tanisha pushed past the boys and went into the house.

"You shouldn't have been smoking!" Duncan shouted.

She slammed the door behind her, leaving Duncan and Flinch alone with TJ's unconscious lump of a body.

"The Creature has spoken," Flinch said.

Duncan shook his head and looked through the back

window at his family. Avery was still searching the paper, Aiah was reading a book, and Tanisha was quietly crying in front of the kitchen sink. Her words felt like heavy weights his body could not carry.

"She's right."

"No, *muchacho*."

"I'm not like them," Duncan said. "I'm much smarter than everyone in my family. Half the time they don't understand a word I'm saying. And then there's all the spy stuff on top of that. They have no idea what to make of me."

"Your family loves you," Flinch said. "The Creature is just angry she got caught."

"Look around, Flinch. My whole family was uprooted from the neighborhood my parents grew up in just so I can get a better education. No one asked her if she wanted to come. No wonder she's angry. She lost her friends, everyone she knows. She's alone, all because her brother is some supposed genius."

Flinch shook his head but offered no argument.

"I have to face facts. I'm a nerd at school and a nerd at home," Duncan said. "Worse, I don't even have a cool secret life anymore. Brand isn't going to send any of us out without our upgrades."

Dejected, Duncan sat down on the stoop, and Flinch joined him. The boys were quiet for a long time until they were both startled by a loud bang in the neighbor's yard. They rushed to the fence to see what was going on. What they saw was a thirty-seven-year-old man floundering in a pile of garbage bags. He had red hair and one too many chins. The poor guy had clearly stumbled into his trash can and sent its contents everywhere. He cursed as he dragged himself to his feet.

"Well, it could be worse," Flinch said. "You could be this guy."

"Mrs. Nesbitt's son, Albert," Duncan said. "I think."

"What do you mean you think?"

"I've never seen him before. He lives in her basement and rarely comes outside. Some of the neighborhood kids think he doesn't even exist. He's like Bigfoot."

"He's a disaster," Flinch said, but when the man took a candy bar from his pocket and unwrapped it, the boy changed his tune. "Though he has excellent taste in chocolate."

Flinch looked at Duncan. "Didn't you say the guy at the bank in Scotland was overweight and had red hair?" Flinch asked.

Duncan stared at the figure. When he tried to imagine Albert in a black-and-green supersuit, he realized the resemblance was uncanny.

"Flinch, I think my neighbor is a supervillain," Duncan whispered.

8

38°53 N, 77°05 W

Mama was very surprised to
get visitors so late at night, but when you open the door and
find the most handsome man you've ever seen standing there,
it's OK to let him in and answer his questions. Of course, she
could have done without the blonde who came with him.

"Is Albert in some kind of trouble, Agent . . . ?"

"Brand. Alexander Brand, Mrs. Nesbitt," the agent said.

"Oh, it's Ms. Nesbitt, Alexander. I'm not married," she said as an excited giggle escaped her mouth.

"We're just curious about where he might have been yesterday, say, around two o'clock in the afternoon?" the blonde woman said.

Mama frowned at the woman's question and kept her focus on Brand's rugged face as she answered. "If I had to lay money on it, I'd say he was locked up in his room with his funny books. Such a shame, really. I had hopes he'd be a great scientist. He had such a way with computers and machines when he was young. But what's a mother to do? The poor boy needs a father figure, you know." She smiled at Brand.

Brand cocked an eyebrow. "I have a couple of questions I'd like to ask him."

Mama thought. "On second thought, he's probably at the comic book shop. He spends all his money on those silly things. Can you imagine? A grown man reading such drivel."

"Is there any chance we might take a look at his room?" the blonde asked.

Mama frowned. Why couldn't this woman leave them be? She and the handsome agent were really hitting it off. "I don't think I should without him here. I tossed out some of his things once when he was a kid and he's been locked down there in the basement for twenty-two years. Maybe when he gets back. He's usually home around ten o'clock."

Brand stood up and his companion followed. "We'll come back then, Ms. Nesbitt."

"Please, call me Gertrude," Mama said.

Brand nodded and then he and his partner left. Mama watched them get into a black sedan and drive away. Once they were gone, Mama rushed to the basement door and pressed her ear against it. Albert was down there. She could hear the annoying beeps and buzzes of his silly movies about wars in space.

She knocked but there was no answer.

"Albert, this is your Mama. I want to see you right now."

"I'm sleeping," his lazy voice complained.

"Albert Nesbitt! You better march your behind up those steps and open this door on the double!"

There was no sound and, after a few moments, Mama knew more drastic measures were needed. She rushed to retrieve her toolbox, hefted it onto the table, and opened the lid. She took a hammer and returned to the door. With all her strength, she smacked the doorknob as hard as she could. Again and again she swung until eventually the knob broke off, taking the lock with it. The door opened. A wave of body odor and stale pizza rushed up the stairs to meet her. Mama hesitated, then ran back to the sink cabinet, found a can of disinfectant spray, and blasted a cloud down the stairs. She hurried down the steps and found her son hunched over a desk, working on an odd device that looked like something out of a science fiction film.

"Albert!" she shouted.

Her son started and spun around.

"Mama! This is my room!"

"Someone from the FBI or the CIA was here asking about you, Albert," Mama said.

"Which one? The FBI or the CIA?"

"Does it matter?" Mama cried. "They told me they think you're in trouble. They want to know what you've been doing with yourself."

"It's no one's business but my own."

Mama scanned the room. There were computer parts scattered everywhere and the walls were lined with schematics for a strange machine. There was a bizarre black-and-green suit lying on Albert's bed and comic books were thrown about willy-nilly.

"Tell me," she said. "Are you in trouble?"

Albert tilted his head back as if pondering her question. "Yes, I guess I am."

"What kind of trouble?"

Albert took a deep breath. "I'm working for an evil genius who is bent on destroying his former friends and then taking over the world using a machine that can hypnotize other machines."

Mama blanched and started to cry. "You've finally gone crazy."

Albert rose from his chair. He snatched his ray gun off the

desk and gave it to her. "No, Mama. I'm fine. This is what I'm building. It's a computer disrupter. It can literally control anything. Televisions, computers, cell phones—anything with a processor. If you aim it at an ATM, it will happily cough up all its money. Even the price scanner at the grocery store can be forced to obey you."

"And what does this evil genius of yours intend to do with it?" Mama demanded.

"He wants to control the world's computer technology," Albert said. "But he's after some old teammates first. He's kind of obsessed with destroying them."

"And what do you get out of it?"

Albert stammered.

Mama could see the answer bouncing around his brain. She knew she would not like what finally escaped.

"Superpowers."

Mama screamed. "Albert, for the love of Pete! Superpowers? How are superpowers going to pay your bills?"

"Well, I'm sure—"

Mama would not hear another word. "No, it's time to be practical. For a device that can take over the world, you should be getting a lot more than eye lasers. What else has your boss offered you?"

"Nothing."

"That's some great negotiation, Albert. Way to make sure you don't get taken advantage of by the boss! Well, lucky for you your mama is here to help. Pack your things, Albert. Pack everything you're going to need to build this machine and every penny you have lying around. We can't stay here anymore. Those agents know you're up to something and they will be back."

"Where are we going?" Albert said as he scooped up a laundry basket of semiclean clothes.

"To talk to your boss about the terms of your *partnership*," Mama said.

The goon did not intimidate Mama. She had faced down Jennifer DiDomizio at the neighborhood bake sale last summer. Jennifer had the audacity to bake lemon squares when she knew full well they were Mama's signature dessert. The two women had screamed at each other so loudly that Bonnie Fuller's chocolate bundt cake collapsed in on itself. If Mama could handle Mrs. DiDomizio's dry and tasteless lemon bars, a guy with a hook for a hand wasn't going to intimidate her.

She climbed right up the rope ladder with her son following sheepishly behind and found Simon sitting in his chair surrounded by squirrels.

"Are you the one taking advantage of my son?"

Simon set down his bag of nuts and sat up in his chair. He eyed her closely. It was clear to Mama the boy was not used to being confronted.

"Excuse me?"

"My son, Albert, says you hired him to build a doomsday device and all you're offering him are some silly superpowers," Mama said.

"I'd hardly call superpowers silly," Simon replied. "When all is said and done, your son might be able to fly or lift a car over his head. He might have heat vision."

"Albert does not need heat vision. What he needs is a future."

"Mom, you're embarrassing me," Albert whined.

"Hush, honey. The grown-ups are talking," Mama snapped, then turned her attention back to Simon. "My son has squandered the last twenty years of his life on comic books, and now he is finally doing something that could turn it all around."

Simon frowned.

Mama reached over and snatched Albert's machine from his hands. "Let's be honest. You can't take over the world with that little pop gun he built."

"That's the prototype, Mama," Albert cried.

"Albert, it's clear that your mother understands exactly what is going on. So, yes, Ms. Nesbitt, now that we know it works, I intend to have Albert build one a thousand times bigger that we can aim at the planet from space. One little zap and every machine from here to Australia will be under my control."

"That should be worth more than being able to leap tall buildings."

"What are you proposing, Ms. Nesbitt?" Simon asked. One of the squirrels climbed up in his lap and then onto his shoulder. It hunched forward as if it too wanted to hear what the strange woman wanted.

"Call me Mama," she said.

"OK, Mama," Simon replied.

"Let's just say that Albert builds you something that lets you take over the entire world."

"Let's say that."

"The world is a big place. It would be hard to manage it all by yourself. You might want to give some of it away just to avoid the headaches. Who better to take that problem off your hands than my son?"

Simon frowned. "When you say 'some of it,' I assume you have specific places in mind."

"I've taken the liberty of making a list," Mama said, handing Simon a slip of paper.

He scanned it. "You want your son to control half the United States, including Arlington, Virginia?"

Mama nodded. "Yes."

"Why Arlington?"

"What's the point of having a son who helped take over the world if you can't brag to the neighbors?"

9

Duncan's fifth-grade teacher, Mr. Pfeiffer, was not good at his job. He spent too little time teaching and too much time talking about his personal life. He rambled on and on about lifting weights, his steady stream of girlfriends and how he had been in a commercial for toilet paper when he was a baby. He knew nearly nothing about anything. He once told his class Abraham Lincoln had died when he slipped in the shower. Most of his students and, if he was honest, he himself, wondered how he had gotten a job as a teacher. After all, he didn't even have a teaching certificate. But Duncan and his teammates knew that it was Pfeiffer's lack of focus that made him the perfect man to teach a group of secret agents who were frequently absent from his class.

"The key to looking strong is not about lifting heavy weights, kids," Pfeiffer said as he rolled up his sleeve to show his biceps. "It's lifting light weights and doing lots of repetitions.

Also, you can't forget the three magic words—protein, protein, and protein."

As Duncan struggled to stay awake, he heard a familiar voice in his head. Mr. Brand was calling. "Team, we need you in the Playground on the double."

Duncan looked over at Matilda. Now that Heathcliff and his mind-bending incisors were gone, it was up to her to come up with a way to distract the class.

"Hey, everybody!" Matilda cried. "There's a pony outside!"

The entire class, with Mr. Pfeiffer in tow, raced to the windows to see. Matilda always found a clever way to get them out of their seats. Duncan marveled at her imagination as he raced with the others to the lockers.

In no time, the team was plopping into their leather chairs, present and accounted for in the Playground.

"We're sending you out," Agent Brand said.

Duncan could feel panic rising in his belly. "Out?"

"Yes, nothing too dangerous. Just a little evidence collecting," Brand said. "Your and Flinch's tip about our mystery villain appears to be correct. After Ms. Holiday and I spoke to his mother, our suspect flew the coop. We need you to go and search his place for anything that will lead us to Simon."

"But—"

"Yes, Gluestick?"

"Our upgrades are down," Duncan cried.

Agent Brand looked as angry as Duncan had ever seen him. "You've been trained as secret agents, correct?"

"Yes."

"And you've been on evidence-collecting missions before, correct?"

"Yes."

"This will be easy, D," Flinch said.

"It's just, our upgrades make us—"

Brand leaned in closely. "If you need some fancy gadgets to make you feel better, we have a whole room full of them. Otherwise, take your team to Albert Nesbitt's house and collect some evidence."

"Albert and his mother must have disappeared in the night," Ruby said as she and the rest of the team walked down into Albert Nesbitt's basement lair. "Ugh, this is where he slept. My whole body is itchy. I'm allergic to sweat and desperation."

"Well, I'm humiliated," Matilda said as she used a broom handle to move a pair of dirty socks. "Now that we're off-line, Brand's giving us jobs for babies. How many times do we have to save the world before we get a little respect?"

Duncan was too busy navigating the stairs to speak. He was loaded down with gizmos. He had taken Agent Brand's advice seriously and packed his pockets with all manner of electronic tools. He needed Flinch's help down the stairs, but he was ready for whatever might occur.

"Gluestick, can I have a chat with you?" Braceface said as he pulled the boy aside.

"Sure, what is it?"

"That little speech Brand was giving in the Playground before we left. You know he was trying to teach you something, right?"

Duncan blinked. He had no idea what his teammate was telling him.

Jackson smiled sympathetically. "Pal, that speech was what we used to call the 'man-up' speech when I played peewee football.

"Man up?"

"Yeah, it's a speech coaches give players who are crying and whining."

"I wasn't—"

"Yes, you were," Jackson interrupted him. "He wasn't telling you that you should carry off every device they have in the HQ. He was telling you that you didn't need them to do your job. In fact, he was telling you that you are perfectly fine to do this mission and that you should stop blubbering about your upgrades."

"Oh."

"It's OK," Jackson said. "Everyone gets the man-up speech

once or twice in their lives. I've just never met anyone who didn't understand it was a man-up speech."

Duncan looked at his teammates. They were all nodding in agreement.

"I've disappointed him, then," Duncan said as he looked down at all his gadgets.

"A little," Matilda said.

"And I'm going to give you my own man-up speech, right now," Ruby said. "Brand is nervous about sending us to do anything. Heathcliff's betrayal hit him like a ton of bricks. He's questioning his decisions and his leadership now. On top of that, the big mistake at the Bank of Scotland has him wondering if we can get the job done. He has the power to dismantle this team, Gluestick. He could refuse to replace our upgrades and send us back to class to be normal. If we want to continue to be the coolest geeks in the world, we all need to show him that we can get the job done, powers or no powers."

Duncan frowned. "But technology is part of what we do. Without it, we wouldn't be able to do half of the cool stuff we've done. Without technology we wouldn't have the Schnoz Projector."

Duncan took out what looked like a pair of novelty glasses complete with a big, goofy nose and bushy mustache. He slipped them onto his face.

"Gluestick, sometimes I worry about you," Matilda said.

"This is no joke," Duncan said. "This is the latest in sensory data collection."

"Sensory what?" Jackson asked.

"It's a new science in which you can collect one sense and transform it into another. The Schnoz Projector collects smells and transmits them into images."

"So if I farted, you would be able to see it?" Flinch cried.

"Um, sadly, yes," Duncan said. "It detects things like perspiration, perfumes, deodorants—any kind of body smell either natural or manmade—and it can show us a crude representation of who it belonged to. It can track the trail of scent around this room, and maybe show us what Albert was doing down here. I've seen the prototype in the Playground and it's amazing. Watch!"

Duncan flipped a button on the side of his glasses and the lenses glowed. A moment later the group heard loud sniffing and then a bright beam of light appeared, revealing a shaky image of Albert.

"Awesome!" Flinch said.

Another wavy figure appeared in the room. She was short with a bun of hair. "Albert's mom wears a lot of perfume and her clothes are dried with fabric softener sheets. She produces a smell that we can trace and, now, even see," Duncan said.

The team watched the two holograms moving about the

room. Though it wasn't a perfect image, you could see they were arguing. Then something unusual happened. Albert rushed to an empty desk and lifted something metallic. Duncan knew it at once. It was the weapon Albert had used on him.

"That's the ray gun! Albert must have built it down here," Matilda said as she watched the images flicker around the room. "His mother doesn't look too happy about it. Look! She's pulling suitcases out of the closet. She's forcing him to pack."

Ruby shook her head in disgust. "She should have turned him in—he's dangerous."

"What's he doing?" Jackson said. The holographic Albert had rushed to a table and appeared to be snatching something from it, but his mother stomped over to him and ripped it from his hands.

Flinch crossed the room to where the two figures had once stood and picked up a stack of comics. "Looks like mommy wasn't happy about what her son wanted to pack."

"Too bad the Schnoz Projector doesn't let us hear what they were saying," Matilda replied. "Is there any chance it will show us where they went?"

"Sorry, the Schnoz Projector works best in enclosed spaces. The wind outside has probably blown away their scents."

"Well, we know for sure that his mother helped him escape," Jackson said as he looked under the bed. "And we know that they packed, so they aren't coming back. Looks like we can turn off the fancy gadget. This is going to require some old-fashioned detective work. Nothing under here but cupcake wrappers and empty juice boxes."

"Any unopened?" Flinch said. "I'm starving!"

Duncan shook his head. "Remember what Benjamin told you: Cut down on the sweets until your upgrades are working again."

Flinch frowned.

Matilda looked through Albert's closet. "I have never met anyone who had so many T-shirts with superhero logos on them."

Ruby searched the dresser drawers. "He's not the cleanest guy. I think he wears his clothes and shoves them back into his drawers."

"Wait, what's this?" Jackson said. He stood up holding a tube of paper in his hands. He took it over to a small table and unrolled it. There was a drawing of Albert in his black-and-green Captain Justice outfit. Unlike the real Albert, this one was muscle-bound and handsome. In his hand was the weapon he had turned on the children.

"This guy has a huge imagination," Matilda said.

"Or there isn't a single mirror in this house," Ruby said.

"He's not a bad artist," Jackson said. "That ray gun looks just like the real thing."

Duncan sighed. "There's so much stuff back at the Playground that could help us. I know one of the scientists was building a device that detects footprints. Benjamin could also track the last days' worth of phone calls."

Ruby frowned. "Come on, Duncan, use your eyeballs for once!" she snapped.

Duncan was stunned. It was clear she was fed up with him. Ruby was often annoyed with Flinch and couldn't stand Jackson, but she'd always treated Duncan with respect. It felt like the whole world had suddenly turned on him.

As the other children searched every nook and cranny of Albert's room for a clue to where the man went, Duncan hesitated, unsure of where to start. He was about to give up when he glanced down at the stack of comics that had meant so much to Albert. His gaze caught on the cover of the comic on top. He snatched it off the pile and stared at it, hardly believing his eyes.

"Look!"

When his teammates turned, he flashed the comic's cover at them.

"*Ultraforce* 119. I haven't read that one," Flinch said.

"No! Look at the guy on the cover. Look at what he's holding in his hand."

Ruby peered at the cover and her eyes got big. "It's Albert's ray gun. He got his idea out of a comic book!"

END TRANSMISSION.

SO FAR, YOU'VE LEARNED
TO CREATE AND DECIPHER
YOUR OWN CODES, AND IN
THE PROCESS YOU'VE LEARNED
SOME VALUABLE LESSONS
ABOUT PERSONAL HYGIENE.
BUT THERE'S MORE TO CODES
THAN LETTER WHEELS. IN FACT,
THERE ARE LOTS OF WAYS TO
SEND A SECRET MESSAGE. SOME
SPIES USE INVISIBLE INK, AND
I'M GOING TO SHOW YOU HOW
TO MAKE IT. ISN'T THAT COOL?
WHY, YOU PROBABLY THOUGHT
THE PRICE OF THIS BOOK WAS
OUTRAGEOUS, BUT LOOK AT
ALL THE PRACTICAL STUFF
I'M TEACHING YOU!

HMM, MAYBE WE SHOULD CHARGE
MORE . . .

OK, TO MAKE INVISIBLE INK YOU'RE GOING TO NEED SOME INGREDIENTS. UNFORTUNATELY, THE INGREDIENTS ARE ALSO INVISIBLE.

WOW, YOU ARE GULLIBLE.

HERE'S WHAT YOU'RE GOING TO NEED:

- A PAN AND A STOVE
- CORNSTARCH
- WATER
- COTTON SWABS
- PAPER
- IODINE
- A SMALL SPONGE

NOW, BEFORE WE MAKE THE INVISIBLE INK, I NEED TO TEST YOU TO MAKE SURE YOU HAVE THE BRAINPOWER TO ACTUALLY DO THIS.

QUESTION 1:
IF I USE THE STOVE WITHOUT
MY PARENTS' SUPERVISION,
I COULD:

- BURN THE HOUSE DOWN
- BURN THE HOUSE DOWN
- BURN THE HOUSE DOWN
- ALL OF THE ABOVE

IF YOU GUESSED ANY OF THE
ANSWERS ABOVE, YOU ARE NOT A
MORON AND THUS WILL KNOW TO
MAKE SURE YOUR PARENTS ARE
WATCHING YOU WHILE YOU COOK
ON THE STOVE. IF YOU GOT THIS
QUESTION WRONG, YOU ARE A
MORON. YOUR PARENTS PROBABLY
ALREADY KNOW THIS. YOU SHOULD
STEER CLEAR OF THE STOVE, AND
FIRE IN GENERAL.

ALL RIGHT, BRAINIAC, LET'S
MAKE US SOME INVISIBLE INK.

MIX 3 TABLESPOONS OF
CORNSTARCH AND 1/4 CUP OF
WATER IN A PAN AND STIR UNTIL
THE CORNSTARCH IS DISSOLVED.
COOK ON LOW HEAT UNDER
A PARENT'S CAREFUL EYE.
ARE YOUR PARENTS AROUND? GOOD.
LET IT COOL FOR A FEW MINUTES,
THEN DIP A COTTON SWAB OR Q-TIP
INTO THE SOLUTION AND WRITE A
SECRET MESSAGE ON A PIECE OF
PAPER. NOW, IN A BOWL, MIX 3
TEASPOONS OF IODINE WITH 2/3 CUP
OF WATER. DIP YOUR SPONGE INTO
IT, MAKING SURE TO SQUEEZE OUT
EXCESS WATER. NOW WIPE THE
SPONGE ON YOUR MESSAGE.

IF YOU FOLLOWED THE
DIRECTIONS EXACTLY,
THEN YOU SHOULD SEE
YOUR MESSAGE IN
PURPLE. IF NOT, WELL,
I DON'T KNOW. I MEAN,
I CAN ONLY DO SO MUCH.

LEVEL 4

ACCESS GRANTED

BEGIN TRANSMISSION:

10

Spencer de La Peña was a novelist. For the last five years of his life, he got up in the morning, ate an egg-white omelet, and bicycled to the local coffee shop on the corner of Wykoff Avenue and Smith Street in Brooklyn. All day long he drank from a bottomless cup of coffee and worked on a sweeping epic about the last days of feudal China. It was a complicated and demanding story with hundreds of characters and thus far had not found a publisher—but it would! Spencer was convinced.

He would write the whole day, and at five o'clock sharp, with his hands so shaky from the caffeine he could barely type, he would file away his novel and go to work on the job that paid his bills—writing comic books.

Spencer was currently working on three titles at the same time: *Sgt. Blast*, *Ultraforce*, and *Clash of Heroes*. Each one was filled with costumed guys who punched one another in the mouth a lot. He had come to comics hoping to give them some depth, but after only a few issues of his retelling of Medea, his editor informed him that readers were not interested in depth. They wanted more punches to the mouth. But hey, it paid the bills.

"Are you Spencer de La Peña?" a voice asked now from beyond his laptop screen. Standing before him was one of the most awkward kids he had ever seen—chubby, short, with purple pants and a clashing shirt. Spencer knew something about awkward kids. He had a huge audience of young readers, all of whom were nervous, ill-adjusted, and destined for a lifetime of bullying.

Spencer frowned. "Sorry, kid, I'm busy writing. I don't have time for autographs."

"I'm not interested in getting one. Are you the guy who writes *Ultraforce?*" the boy said. He held out a copy of the comic.

"Yes, and—"

"Did you write this one?"

The writer eyed the cover. It was an issue he had written featuring a character he had created himself—the Machine Master.

"Yeah."

The boy pointed to the villain's weapon—a space-age ray

gun that made machines bend to the villain's every whim. "How does this work?"

Spencer rolled his eyes. He scooped up his computer and snatched his jacket. "Kid, I know all this stuff is very interesting, and I admit to being a bit of a fanboy myself, but nothing in those pages is real. That ray gun doesn't exist, and if you built it it wouldn't work. I made it up. It's imagination. So, I've got to get going. It was nice to meet you, but I have a deadline."

"But—"

"I'm sure there's some online community about this comic. Perhaps if you all put your heads together, you can figure it out for yourselves." He walked out of the shop. Unfortunately, his path was blocked by four more equally geeky kids.

"I don't think you answered my friend's question," a jittery Mexican kid said.

"What is this? Are you kids part of some fan club?"

"Something like that," the boy from inside the coffee shop said as he joined them. "And we need your help."

Suddenly, Spencer felt a little sting on his hand. When he looked down, he noticed that a boy with huge braces had given him an injection. Before he could complain, he felt a tremendous wave of sleepiness and then everything went black.

When he woke up, Spencer had no idea how long he had been asleep. He also had no idea how he had strapped himself into a leather chair on what looked like a very fancy airplane. He also had no idea who the beautiful woman was who was standing over him, but she made the first two mysteries seem like a lot less of a problem.

"Good evening, Mr. La Peña," the woman said. "My name is Ms. Holiday, and you're on board the School Bus."

"It's been a while since I was in school, but I'm pretty sure it hasn't been long enough for them to swap out buses for planes."

Ms. Holiday smiled. "Actually, you're not on a plane, Spencer." She pointed out the tiny window to his right. He glanced over, then did a double take. Outside he could see the planet Earth. It was very far away and getting smaller by the second. Still, he would bet that people heard him screaming all the way from space.

"What is going on? Why have you shot me into space?" he said after he finally calmed down.

"Because what we have to tell you is unbelievable," a voice said from behind him. Spencer swiveled his chair around. Behind him were the dorky kids from the coffee shop. The chubby black kid was speaking. "And we really don't have time to explain it. Let's just say we're secret agents, we work for the government, this is our space jet, and we need your help."

"You're a bunch of—"

"Kids?" the little Korean girl with the unibrow asked. "Yeah, we get that a lot. But, again, we're spies. The rest of it is classified, Spencer, so let us get to the point."

The girl with the glasses and puffy hair was next. "There's a very bad man who has invented a machine inspired by your comic book."

"That's crazy."

"Don't interrupt or I will have my friend toss you out the door," the puffy-haired girl said, gesturing to the jittery Mexican kid, who did a strongman pose. "Now, this very bad man has already used this device to rob a bank and to damage some very powerful . . . weapons. We believe he is working for an even badder man than himself."

"What has that got to do with me?" Spencer said. He

thought he might hyperventilate at the weirdness of it all. The lady offered him a drink of water.

"You think I helped him?" he asked when he had calmed down a bit.

"No," the little Korean girl said. "We think he got the idea from you."

"I can't be responsible for—"

"Mr. La Peña," the chubby kid interrupted. "We are not accusing you of being a bad guy. We are just trying to find out how this ray gun you imagined works. The guy who built the real-life version intends to build a much bigger version, which could lead to a very big problem. If he succeeds, he and his employer could easily upset the balance

of power in every corner of the world. So, again, I know this is confusing—"

"And freaky," the Mexican kid said with a laugh.

"You kids are nuts," Spencer cried, trying to break his restraints. "You can't pull some silly gadget out of a comic book and make it real."

The woman pointed at a bank of computer screens. "Benjamin, can you show our guest the footage of Albert's robbery?"

A moment later the screens showed pictures of an obese man in a costume. His ray gun was pointed directly at the bank manager, who cowered beneath her desk.

"It's . . . it's real," Spencer stammered.

"How does it work?" the girl with the puffy hair asked impatiently.

"If that guy got his ideas from my comics, I want you to be clear that I just made it all up. I'm no scientist. It's just, well, I was reading this article about nanobyte technology in a science magazine. You know nanobytes? Those tiny microscopic robots?"

The children shared a knowing look. "We've heard of them," the chubby kid said.

"There was a theory that they could use the robots for a variety of different tasks, everything from faster computers to brain surgery. I started wondering if these robots might be susceptible to computer viruses, so I thought that a cool villain might be a guy who manipulates machines by making them sick."

"How does he do that?" the Korean girl asked.

"Again, I'm not an expert, but I did do a little research. When a computer gets a virus, it's because it downloaded something designed to make it sick, but you can't just download things into microwaves and cars and stuff. So how do you get the virus into the machine without the download? You send it through the air. Machine Master's gun is really just a portable wireless connection that beams viruses into machines. The ray gun turns the virus into a radio wave and fires it. The target machine is bombarded with a virus, new information—whatever. Most machines aren't designed to fight back. You could use this ray gun to completely reprogram anything with a processor."

"Like hypnotizing it," the puffy-haired girl said.

Spencer nodded. "Yeah, I guess so."

"What kind of materials would you need to build one that could take over all the world's machines at once?" the chubby kid said.

"That would be impossible," Spencer said.

"Imagine it's not," the Mexican kid said. "Imagine you had all the money in the world, all the workers you needed, and a giant brain that could put it all together."

"One, you would need an infrared crystal to transmit the signal."

"Can we bring the language down to those who are still in elementary school?" the kid with braces complained from the cockpit.

"What I'm saying is that if you have ever seen a remote control, the part where the beam comes out is usually a piece of glass or plastic that directs the signal. A tiny diamond works even better. If you were going to build a huge machine, you'd probably need a big diamond to keep it stable—actually, a really big diamond. Secondly, you would need an incredible number of computer chips and processors . . . and, lastly, to affect every machine on Earth, you would have to get your ray gun high enough into orbit to hit the whole planet at once."

"Mr. La Peña, I appreciate your time," the puffy-haired girl said.

"Can we send him home?" the lovely woman said. "He looks like he's had a long day."

The girl nodded.

Ms. Holiday smiled and held out her hand. Spencer took it and a tingling feeling raced through him. He'd never been near someone so pretty.

"It was very nice to meet you, Ms. Holiday," he said.

"Perhaps we could get together sometime. You know, I have an extra ticket to Comic Con."

Ms. Holiday blushed and Spencer felt a jolt. Then he looked down and realized the woman had injected him with something, just like the kids had at the coffee shop.

"Aww man," he said, but he was asleep before he could say anything else.

The next morning he woke up in his apartment, curled up in bed, feeling as if he had had the best night of sleep of his life. He sat up, rubbed the sand from his eyes, and felt an incredible rush of inspiration roll over him. He darted to his phone and dialed his editor at the comic book company.

"Pete, this is Spencer," he said excitedly. "Pete, just listen to me. I have the best idea for a comic book ever! It's about these five kids. They work for the government and they have this very hot woman overseeing them. They ride around in a rocket and . . . what am I calling it? I haven't figured it out yet, but it's my next project. What? Forget about the novel. Feudal China can wait!"

11

38°53 N, 77°05 W

Albert had a routine. Every day he woke up at the crack of 2:00 PM. He would eat a breakfast of whatever fast food he had not finished the night before. Then he would take a nap.

At 4:00 he would wake and watch a series of courtroom shows featuring sassy but fair judges. He particularly enjoyed Judge Creole, who was Cajun and had a spicy personality to match. At 6:00 he would stagger out of the basement and head to the comic shop to either buy new books or just hang out. At 10:00 he would head back home to watch whatever science fiction television show he had taped and eat something that came from a can and could be cooked in the microwave.

But his whole routine was turned upside-down now that he had a job. His day started whenever the squirrels began scampering around the trees, snapping and screeching at one another, and knocking pinecones down on his head. This was usually around 5:00 AM. His mama was usually up by then preparing a breakfast of fruit, whole grain bread, and sugar-free oatmeal. It made him gag. Simon and his goon would join them, and they would talk about things in the news, the weather, and their diabolical plans for crushing the spirit of everyone on the planet. Albert found it tedious. He did not feel much like socializing in the morning, let alone eating a wholesome breakfast.

Then Simon and his paid muscle, along with the squirrels, would climb out of the tree fortress and set off to rob a bank, leaving Albert alone with his mother. This was the part of the day that Albert really hated.

"I tell you, Albert. You are ten thousand times smarter than that kid. Does he really think he can rule the world? You should be in charge of this whole operation," his mama said.

"Mama, it's his plan and he's paying for everything," Albert argued.

Mama shrugged. "A waste of money if you ask me. Albert, I appreciate your loyalty but I'm just saying, if you hear someone knocking on the door, that's opportunity."

"Are you telling me I should betray him?"

"Shhhhhhhh!" Mama cried. "You have no idea if one of those furry little tree rats is up in the branches. I swear they understand him when he talks."

"Mama, I don't want to talk about this anymore," Albert said. "You're meddling, just like you did when I was a kid."

"I never meddled!"

Albert was stunned. "Mama, you had your finger in everything I did. All the pushing to be a scientist. Well, here I am, a scientist, and now that's not enough. I don't want to take over the world. I want to save it."

"You are so naive," Mama said, slamming her pot of oatmeal down on the table. "What kind of money does a superhero make? Is there a retirement plan? Do you get medical insurance? Dental? Do you even get a parking space or a cubicle? We're talking about the future, Albert! You are almost forty years old. You can either buckle down with a job that will give you control over the whole world or run around in long underwear wondering how you're going to pay the gas bill!"

Albert frowned. His mama just didn't understand, but that's not what bothered him. He had been dreaming about being a hero for twenty-five years, and in only a few short days he had turned to a life of crime. Ruling the world? The thought made him shudder. Had he really sunk that low? He was no better than Two-Face or Lex Luthor. He was helping an evil genius. Simon shouldn't have been his employer. He should have been his nemesis.

Albert pushed his disappointment from his mind and

flipped on his computer. He had to get to work, and today he was on the hunt. He typed the word "diamonds" into the search engine. For the weapon, he needed enough diamonds to fill a truck.

Results came up—mostly references to the late Marilyn Monroe and an actress named Zsa Zsa Gabor. But as Albert scrolled down, he found something truly interesting. He clicked on it and found that there was a collection of giant diamonds just waiting to be snatched. But as he read further, he discovered something very uncomfortable.

"Mama, I found parts for the big ray gun," he said.

Mama clapped. "I knew you would. How do we get them?"

"I'm going to have to learn to swim."

38°53 N, 77°05 W

Duncan stood in his bedroom,
Benjamin hovering patiently around his head.

"Gluestick?" the orb buzzed. "I asked you if you wanted your usual set of clothing."

"Yes, I know, I'm . . . thinking," Duncan said.

"Might I ask what you are thinking about?"

Duncan studied a picture of his family that hung on the wall. They all looked so normal, except for him. "Changing my style."

The little blue orb seemed surprised. "You have a style?"

Duncan sighed. "Benjamin, do you think I'm awkward?"

"I am aware that you and the team share a certain number of social obstacles, but as a computer it is difficult to process why that might be a problem. I've come to understand that you are frequently teased, but you mustn't forget that being a nerd is a big part of your cover story. Your awkwardness keeps people from paying too much attention to you so that your duties as a spy are not hindered."

"Oh, if we humans only thought like you—all processors and logic. But the thing is, I've been used to being a nerd for a while now. At school kids have been calling me a geek since I was five. It never really bothered me because I felt like I was different for a reason. I also knew that I could go home after school and be someplace where people thought I was great . . . I never thought I'd be a misfit here, too."

The orb blinked at him.

"Tanisha says I'm not like the rest of the family. She says I don't fit in here."

"I've been told that human beings frequently say and do things they regret when they are angry. I'm sure the Creature will apologize to you soon."

"No, I don't think she will," Duncan said. He'd seen her a dozen times since the incident with TJ, and she wouldn't even look at him.

"Well, don't make too much of it. There are plenty of people who think you fit in just fine. Still, a little wardrobe update might do you good," the orb said.

Suddenly, rolls of fabric were unfolding out of the wall and the sounds of scissors and tape filled the air.

In no time, Duncan stepped out of his room only to walk

smack into the Creature. Tanisha snarled at him, then eyed him up and down.

"What are you dressed as?" she said.

"Just trying to fit in." Duncan looked down at his outfit. He had on a red polo shirt with blue jeans and high-top sneakers. His shirt fit and his pants went all the way down to his shoes. He looked like nearly every kid at his school. He smiled and padded down the hall into the kitchen, where his father was fighting with the toaster and his mother was enjoying some coffee. The Creature followed him.

Avery and Aiah stared at Duncan in disbelief.

"What?" Duncan said, defensively.

Aiah stammered. "You look . . . handsome."

"Yes, Halloween has come early," the Creature said.

Avery frowned at his daughter. "You know, when you open your mouth, sometimes very terrible things come out. We don't talk to family this way."

Tanisha stared at her father, then broke into tears and raced out of the room.

"Was I too hard on her?" Avery asked his wife.

Aiah shook her head. "She's going through something. I'll talk to her later."

Suddenly, there was a buzz in Duncan's nose and he sneezed.

"Is that a cold or a mission?" Aiah asked.

"I need a ride to school," Duncan said. "As fast as we can get there."

Two hours later Duncan stood shivering in his short-sleeved polo on the deck of the S.S. *Julia Child* staring at a submersible. He had seen similar crafts in documentaries about seafloor exploration, but had never seen one up close. The podlike submersible had a half-globe window made from superstrong transparent plastic and two circulating fins that moved the machine through the water. There were dozens of high-powered lights attached to the outside, as well as half a dozen cameras that could catch images in every direction.

"Hello, agents," a tall, thin man said as he stepped onto the deck. His bald head and skin like charcoal made him an intimidating figure, and everyone stopped what they were doing and gave him their full attention.

Agent Brand greeted the man with a handshake. "It's an honor to meet you, Captain Blancard, or may I call you Agent Fishhead?"

Captain Blancard smiled. "It's been a long time since anyone has called me that." He laughed. "I think Adrian will do just fine."

Ruby was sporting a rare smile. "He was a member of NERDS back in the 1970s," she informed her team. It was clear she felt she was in the presence of a rock star. "Fishhead was an amazing spy."

"Why is he here?" Jackson asked. "I thought they retired us when we turn eighteen."

"We keep a few agents on retainer when they go into a line of business that can be helpful," Ms. Holiday explained. "Captain Blancard has gone on to be one of the world's preeminent deep-sea explorers."

"Let's be honest, children. I'm a treasure hunter, and a very good one at that," Blancard said as he smiled at Ms. Holiday.

He turned and gestured at the submersible. "Some might even call me a pirate. But, I ask you, did a pirate ever have such wonderful machines?"

"Sir, I've never seen a submersible with arms," Jackson said.

Ruby cocked an eyebrow. "You know about submersibles?"

"I'm not just a pretty face, you know," Jackson said.

Blancard laughed. "You are right, my friend. Not a lot of submersibles have robotic limbs, but they are useful for picking things up off the ocean floor, and I have found that in the briny deep there are things lurking that might enjoy taking a bite out of you. Some of those things are very, very big. I had these arms designed so I could fight back. Allow me to introduce you all

to your vessel, the *Muhammad Ali*. Floats like a butterfly but stings like a bee."

He pushed a button on a control pad and the two mechanical arms went into action, shadowboxing the air, until coming to a rest.

"Awesome sauce!" Flinch cried.

"I call dibs on the fighting arms," Matilda said.

"Yes, the *Ali*'s a fighter, and strong. Has a shell made from titanium and a Plexiglas window shield that can resist nearly a hundred times the pressure of the surface."

"What's the plan, boss?" Ruby asked Brand.

"I'll leave that to our information specialist," Brand said as he gestured to Ms. Holiday.

"We're three miles above the wreck of the *Bom Jesus*, a Portuguese trading ship that is rumored to have sunk here two hundred and fifty years ago. Among its cargo were silk, spices, and three tons of Portuguese gold. We also believe that the hold contains the Azreal Diamond Cache. Legend has it that the ship was hauling crates of enormous diamonds—some of the biggest the world had ever seen. Miners discovered them on the Ivory Coast and it took a hundred men to get the entire haul aboard the ship," Ms. Holiday said, then turned to Captain Blancard. "Most people believe the diamonds are a myth."

"Most people have no imagination, Lisa," Blancard said with a mighty laugh. "Which is exactly how my men and I have gotten so rich."

Blancard's sailors let out a loud "Boo-yah!"

Agent Brand turned to the children. "The idea here is to take the diamonds before Simon can. No diamonds, no doomsday device. The mission is a little different than most, but all of you have been trained in underwater combat, so it shouldn't be too difficult. Take the *Ali* down to the ocean floor and find the shipwreck."

"Do you think the diamonds are really down there?" Matilda asked.

"Eyewitness reports claim the ship was too heavy to maneuver," Ms. Holiday noted. "It's very likely that the extra weight of the jewels led to its sinking."

"If they are down there, use the submersible to bring them to the surface," Blancard said. "And keep the cameras running at all times. My crew's eyes can spot things of value that you might overlook. That's how we make our living."

"So where are our packs?" Duncan asked the librarian.

"Kids, everything you need for this mission is up here," she said as she tapped her finger against her skull.

"You've got to be—" Duncan cried, but caught Ruby's stern expression reminding him that he was supposed to "man up."

"None of your abilities would do you much good underwater, anyway, bro," Flinch said.

"Blancard will use the radio to guide you in steering the submersible, but I'm told it's quite simple." Ms. Holiday turned her attention to Duncan. "Just remember, you are the best secret agents the world has ever seen. Isn't that right, Alexander?"

Mr. Brand grunted but nodded.

The captain's men helped the children into their seats. Then the vessel was raised off the deck of the *Julia Child*.

"Take care of my sub!" the captain called over the radio.

The *Muhammad Ali* swung over the side of the ship and lowered into the water. Soon, the chains that held the little submersible aloft released and it plopped into the water with a jolt. Not that the team noticed. They were already leaping to their responsibilities. Ruby took control of the onboard computer and the radar device, which was currently tracking a school of dolphins directly below them. Matilda was in charge of the mechanical arms and immediately began throwing practice haymakers and uppercuts. Jackson was getting a feel for the sub's harpoon gun. Flinch was in charge of cameras and spotlights. He rarely blinked and wouldn't miss anything. It was up to Duncan to steer the submersible. He sat in the captain's chair, watching as the waves swallowed the craft.

"So that guy was once in NERDS?" Jackson said.

"Well, he's a total hottie now," Matilda said.

"Gross!" Ruby cried. "He's so old."

"I'm just saying, if he turned out that good-looking, there might be hope for us all."

"Fishhead was on the team from 1973 to 1983," Ruby said. "They called him Fishhead because he was a naturally great swimmer."

"What about his upgrades?" Duncan asked.

"He didn't have any at first," Ruby explained. "They had a crude computer system that suggested gadgets based on a spy's weaknesses. But mostly they were just kids who were really good at something."

As the other kids imagined the prehistoric days of NERDS, the submersible sank farther into the deep. There was no need for Duncan to steer. Gravity was carrying the small craft to the bottom of the ocean. Duncan drifted as well, into his own thoughts: his sister's mean comments, his parents' confused expressions when he spoke, his anxiety over losing his upgrades. Somehow it was all tied together; he just couldn't undo the knot. He didn't like being confused. It made him feel like he used to before he became a spy and his whole life changed—back when he was below average.

"What's on your mind, *muchacho*? And nice threads, by the way," Flinch said as he leaned forward.

"Thanks. Just thinking about our mission," Duncan lied.

"Isn't this great? It's like that book *Twenty Thousand Leagues Under the Sea.* You're like Captain Nemo up here in the control seat. Whoa! Did you see that?"

Duncan looked out the window and saw a fin swim past the submersible. The only problem was, this fin was four times the size of the craft. "What was it?"

"How would I know?" Flinch said, his eyes as big as saucers. "The closest I've ever gotten to the ocean is a box of Swedish Fish."

"It's a whale," Ruby said, following it on her radar screen. "It must weigh close to twenty tons."

"That would make it a whale shark," Duncan said. "It's one of the biggest animals in the world and it's native to this part of the ocean."

"Whale shark?" Jackson cried as he swiveled the harpoon gun to prepare for attack.

"Relax, it's harmless," Duncan said.

The whale shark glided by once more, this time slowing to fix a massive eye on the craft. The children held their breath until the animal swam away, then craned their necks to follow its path. Swimming in its wake were thousands of tiny silver fish. They moved about in a single massive group, less like fish and more like a ribbon of gelatin trailing the whale shark. Suddenly, a school of tuna fish appeared from nowhere, darting in and out of the hitchhikers, feasting on the flickering ribbons of life. Duncan had never seen anything like it in the world.

"Do we not have the best jobs ever?" Flinch cried.

Just then, the front glass flickered and the image of Agent Brand appeared before them all. He looked rather irritated.

"What's the problem, boss man?" Matilda asked. "You look angry."

"Isn't that how he always looks?" Jackson mumbled.

"I'm fine, Wheezer," Brand said, though his irritated voice said otherwise.

"We haven't found anything yet, sir," Ruby said.

"It will take you a half an hour to make it to the spot we believe the *Bom Jesus* settled. I was just letting you know our sonar scans have shown that there is indeed something below you."

"Where's Ms. Holiday?" Duncan asked.

"Ms. Holiday is busy speaking with Captain Blancard," Brand snarled.

"Oooooh," said Matilda. The children shared a knowing look, which seemed to irritate the agent even more. A moment later his image vanished from the glass.

"That poor dumb moron," Matilda said. "He'll lose her if he doesn't learn to talk."

"Ms. Holiday is the bomb," Jackson added.

After some time, Ruby alerted them that they were quickly approaching the ocean floor. Flinch flipped on the external lights and Duncan switched on the motor. He could feel the vibration of pumping engines through his body as the *Ali* suddenly responded to the tiniest movement of the controls. He gripped the throttle and soon the little submersible was propelled forward through the water, just above the seabed.

"See anything out there, Flinch?" Matilda asked. "Rather, see anything I can punch in the face?"

Flinch grinned. "Nothing yet, but you'll be the first to know. Wait! There's something!"

Duncan brought the craft to a halt. "I don't see a thing."

"There," Flinch said, pointing out the window at a green mass on the sandy floor.

"Congrats, you spotted some algae," Jackson said. "Good job, eagle eye."

Flinch laughed. "That's not algae. Well, it is, but what's underneath it isn't algae. That's an anchor."

Ruby's terminal was beeping wildly. "He's right. This computer photographs objects and then allows me to digitally remove surface materials that may have collected on them. That's an anchor all right."

"Then the *Bom Jesus* must be around here somewhere," Matilda said.

Duncan piloted the ship along the sandy floor. Soon they came across some ancient barrels and what looked like a rudder. It wasn't long before they saw the stern of the ship. That's when Matilda let out another little cry.

Duncan tapped the radio. "Agent Brand. Agent Holiday. The *Muhammad Ali* has found the *Bom Jesus*."

Holiday's face appeared on the screen. "Amazing! Perhaps all of you will become treasure hunters one day like Captain Blancard here. Any sign of our diamonds?"

Ruby shrugged. "Nothing yet. We're going to have to get closer."

Duncan steered them closer to the ancient ship. Flinch spotted a huge hole in the hull. From the look of the wreck, the *Bom Jesus* had sunk on its side. Duncan piloted the submersible closer, spotting several cannons poking out of windows and a massive hole on one side of the ship. Duncan couldn't be sure, but it looked as if one of the cannons had exploded, causing the hole and possibly sending the ship down beneath the waves. The hole was just big enough for the *Muhammad Ali* to enter, but the moment Duncan tried, a great white shark charged out of the ship at them, snapping its jaws and causing the children to scream. When the beast found nothing to eat, it circled around, then got bored and slipped away.

Duncan eased the submersible into the ancient ship and Flinch directed the high-powered lights. Inside, nearly everything was covered in a green sludge. Little crabs scurried into crevices and a few striped fish darted away. It was both beautiful and ghostly.

"There's one of the cannons," Flinch said as Duncan steered the ship around the hull. The ancient iron gun sat among little barrels with xxx painted on them.

"Matilda, I think we're going to need those arms," Duncan said. "If the diamonds are here, they're in the bottom of the boat. Pull up the floorboards, but steer clear of those barrels. I suspect they're full of gunpowder."

Matilda grinned as she slipped her hands into two rubber gloves. Suddenly the arms on either side of the craft came to life. Matilda tore into the bottom of the boat, causing algae, plankton, and sand to swirl around the sub.

"I've broken through," Matilda said.

They waited for the swirling fog to settle, only to find the mechanical arms had ripped a hole into a small room. Inside were tables and chairs and two bone-white skeletons that floated up and hit the submersible window. Ruby shrieked but Jackson and Flinch laughed.

"That was awesome!" Flinch cried.

"Look!" Duncan cried.

Scattered about the room were wooden chests with brass padlocks.

The NERDS cheered. It looked as if they had found the diamonds.

Captain Blancard's face reappeared in the glass. "Very good, my friends. Now, Gluestick, there is a button just above your right knee that says TRUNK. Do you see it? Push that button."

Duncan pushed the button and watched as a portion of the submersible rolled out from underneath the craft. Its lid opened, revealing a large storage space.

"OK, Wheezer, let's get one of those chests into the submersible and opened. No point bringing them all up if all we're going to find is some old clothes," Blancard said. "But be gentle. Those chests are hundreds of years old."

Duncan watched as Matilda manipulated the arms until one of the chests was inside the trunk of the sub. Duncan pressed the button again and the trunk retracted, sealing itself tight. Now Jackson hurried to open a trapdoor in the floor of the craft. In a pool of water below them was the chest. After some fiddling with the ancient padlock, Jackson managed to pry the lid open. Inside was one of the biggest diamonds any of them had ever seen.

"The Azreal Cache!" Jackson cried.

"Also known as my early retirement!" Blancard exclaimed. Duncan could hear his men cheering in the background.

Brand reappeared. "OK, team. Let's grab all the chests and get them to the surface on the double. You should be very proud of yourselves. You stopped Simon's plan before it even got started!"

Suddenly, there was a tremendous jolt to the sub and the children were knocked about. Duncan slammed his head into the window.

"What was that?" Matilda said.

Jackson crawled into his harpoon gun chair and swiveled about. "Uh-oh," he said.

Duncan spun the *Ali* around and came nose-to-nose with a second submersible. He could see Simon, Albert Nesbitt, an overgrown man with a hook for a hand, an older woman, and two-dozen squirrels inside.

"He's hailing us," Ruby said. She snarled and flipped a switch.

"Hello, old friends," Simon's voice said. It was filled with rage and bitterness.

"Too late, Heathcliff. The diamonds are ours," Matilda taunted.

"My name is Simon!" the boy bellowed so loudly it shook Duncan's eardrums. "I knew you fools would lead me to the

Azreal diamonds. To be completely honest, we had no idea where they were, but considering Mr. Brand's proactive style, I knew you fools would go hunting for them first and we could just follow you. Now get out of my way."

"Not this time," Flinch said. "If you want them, you're going to have to take them."

"Not a problem," Simon said. "My associate can handle that."

Simon's goon slipped into a set of gloves identical to Matilda's, and suddenly the mechanical arms on Simon's craft came to life. With one punch, the *Muhammad Ali* was thrown backward and crashed through the side of the *Bom Jesus*. Everyone inside the craft was jostled about like popping corn.

"What's going on down there?" Agent Brand cried; his face appeared in the glass again.

"Simon is here and he's after the diamonds," Ruby replied.

"Matilda, time to put your gloves on," Jackson said.

"My pleasure!" Matilda said. Soon she was swinging back at Simon's ship, which had followed theirs out the side of the *Bom Jesus*. The mechanical fist glanced off of Simon's sub, but the force was enough to knock it off balance.

Once Simon's sub had righted itself, the two submersibles traded punches. One devastating blow after another knocked the little ships around at the bottom of the sea.

"I've got a question," Ruby said. "I know the ship can

handle a lot of pressure, but can it take a sucker punch from an identical submersible?" Another punch answered her question. It glanced off the side of the window, leaving a tiny, hairline crack.

"OK, that's bad," Flinch said to Duncan. "How about you get us out of here, buddy?"

Duncan gunned the engines to move the craft backward. But suddenly, a massive explosion from inside the *Bom Jesus* caused the submersible to fly forward, its instruments spinning and buzzing.

"What was that?" Jackson cried.

"Must be some of that gunpowder," Matilda said.

"That's not possible," Ruby cried. "This ship sank more than two hundred years ago. Any gunpowder they had on board could never have survived this long underwater."

There was another explosion, and the tiny craft was knocked about again.

"Tell that to the gunpowder," Flinch said. "I think all this fighting around it is setting it off. We need to get the diamonds and get out of here fast."

"The ship's steering is out of whack!" Duncan cried as Simon's sub closed in.

"Got any ideas, gadget boy?" Jackson shouted to Duncan.

Duncan was at a loss. If he had his abilities, he could shoot a spray of glue into Simon's engines and gunk up the works. But he didn't have any abilities. He was just a kid now. A normal kid who was beginning to have a panic attack. He felt fevered and flushed. Air in the craft seemed harder to come by, and then, suddenly, he knew what to do.

"Hang on," Duncan said. "And hold your breath. I'm venting the compressed oxygen into the ballast tank. It'll push the water out and we will rise fast. I just hope we have enough oxygen to breathe until we get to the surface."

Duncan pushed a button and a red warning light flashed on the controls. A mighty flow of bubbles fired out of the back of the *Muhammad Ali.* It began to rise higher and higher toward the surface, leaving Simon and his gang below.

"Where are we going?" Matilda complained. "I'm not done with him yet!"

"I have no idea how many punches this craft can take, and I think we've had one too many, Wheezer," Duncan said, pointing to the crack in the window. It had grown considerably.

"But what about the rest of the diamonds!" cried Jackson. "Simon will get them."

"Yeah, we can't leave now!" shouted Finch.

"The sub is broken," said Duncan. "There's nothing I can do."

"See ya, NERDS," Simon's voice cackled over the speakers as the submersible rose higher and higher. "Thanks for leaving all these diamonds for me. It's just so convenient that I can predict your moves at every turn."

Brand's face appeared in the glass. "We've been monitoring the situation from above. We'll pick you up on the surface," he said tersely.

Duncan felt his face light up with embarrassment. It was clear Brand was disappointed in them.

"Does someone need a lift?" Blancard's friendly voice said over the communications system a few minutes later, as they bobbed to the surface near the S.S. *Julia Child.*

Duncan tried to smile, but all he could think of was Agent Brand's disappointed face.

END TRANSMISSION.

NICE TO SEE THAT YOU DID
NOT BURN THE HOUSE DOWN.
REALLY. I WAS WORRIED.

ALL RIGHT, NOW LET'S DO
SOME MORE CODE MAKING. YOU MAY
FIND THIS TEDIOUS, BUT THE TRUTH
IS YOU'RE REALLY GOING TO NEED
THIS STUFF WHEN THEY SEND YOU OUT
IN THE FIELD. CODES ARE, LIKE,
A REALLY BIG DEAL. NOW LET'S BUILD
ON WHAT WE LEARNED WITH THE
SUBSTITUTION CIPHER, BUT INSTEAD
OF SUBSTITUTING ONE LETTER FOR
ANOTHER, ALL YOU HAVE TO DO IS
HAVE A CAREFUL EYE.

THIS MESSAGE WAS CREATED
BY A GUY NAMED FRANCIS BACON,
AND THE METHOD IS
SIMPLE—WRITE YOUR SECRET
MESSAGE INSIDE A SECRET MESSAGE.
I CAN SEE THE CONFUSED LOOK
ON YOUR FACE AND NOW REALIZE
THERE IS A DIFFERENCE BETWEEN
THAT FACE AND YOUR REGULAR
FACE. THAT'S A RELIEF.
WHAT I'M SAYING IS, YOU USE
DIFFERENT TYPE FONTS TO HIGHLIGHT
THE REAL SECRET MESSAGE.
FOR INSTANCE, YOU COULD USE
A BOLD FONT FOR THE LETTERS
THAT ARE IMPORTANT TO YOUR
REAL MESSAGE. TRY THIS ONE:

OVER **YO**NDER, **UNDER** THE **F**IR TR**E**ES,
TRACKS WE**RE** FOUND. **T**HE **A**WFUL AND
FOUL AROMA OF THE **SA**BER-TOOTHED
BADGER **A**RISES. VILE **Y**ELPS **SO**AR
UNDER THE **BR**OKEN MOON. T**A**KE
YOUR CHILDREN. RUN
FOR **THE** HILLS.

I DON'T KNOW WHAT'S SCARIER . . . THE MESSAGE OR THE SECRET IT CONTAINS!

LEVEL 5
ACCESS GRANTED
BEGIN TRANSMISSION:

13

"Why didn't you shoot their sub with the harpoon gun?" Mama shrieked at Simon as they puttered toward the surface with their treasure.

"Because I enjoy taunting them with their inadequacies," Simon said.

"But you've let them survive," Mama cried. "Turn this thing around and do the job right."

"Mama!" Albert cried. He could have died from embarrassment.

"I'm just saying, the only way to insure that good guys are no longer a threat to us is to see them die before our eyes."

Albert held his head in his hands and wondered how he had gotten into his current predicament. He was working for a prepubescent lunatic, a walking pile of muscles with a hook for a hand, and his own bloodthirsty mother. Were superpowers worth all this?

Albert couldn't help but think of the kids in the other submersible, fighting for their lives. They were brave. A bunch of kids who couldn't have been older than twelve had tried to save the world. They were the real heroes.

"Albert, you look sad," Mama cried. "We just got a part for your big machine."

"Oh, yeah, that's awesome," Albert said, though he refused to look at her.

When the submersible broke the surface, Mama leaped out of her seat.

"Wait a minute! I've seen that boy!" she cried.

"Which boy?" Simon asked.

"The one who was driving the other sub. He lives right next door to me. His name is Duncan Dewey!"

14

38°53 N, 77°05 W

Duncan was surprised to find the Creature waiting for him in the Playground.

"Dad, he's back," she said, as if disappointed that he'd arrived.

Avery hopped up from a chair with a worried and tired expression on his face. He looked as if he hadn't slept all night.

"Huh?" Duncan said. "How did you all get in here?"

"You're not the only one who is good at spying, Duncan," Tanisha said slyly.

"Oh, thank heavens," Aiah said as she peppered the boy's face with tear-soaked kisses. "I don't think I can handle this anymore, Duncan."

"Mom, I'm fine. What are you talking about?"

"Ms. Nesbitt from next door came over to say she had heard you were in an accident and was very sorry," Aiah said.

Duncan and Flinch shared a knowing look. "Albert's mom!" they said at the same time.

"I thought you had been hurt, or worse," Avery said. "I panicked."

"Duncan is alive and well," Ms. Holiday said as she stepped into the room. "If you would like to take him home that's fine, but unfortunately it will prevent him from receiving his new upgrades today."

Duncan's father spun around on the librarian. "Let me get this straight: You sent my son on a dangerous mission without those things you put in him?"

"He's been fully trained as a—"

"He's a little boy!" Avery shouted. "The last guy who ran this place promised Duncan he would be safe. We only went along with this because we saw that he had been given the equivalent of superpowers. You're telling me you're sending him to die without any of that."

"Duncan is a very capable agent," Ms. Holiday added.

"Two years ago this kid was eating paste for money!" Avery shouted.

"Avery!" his mother cried.

"He what?" the Creature said.

"I'm sorry, son," Avery said. "I brought you to this school

and allowed you to be in this program to give you a chance. You were supposed to be surrounded by geniuses and have access to ideas, technology, science! I didn't bring you here to get killed. You're done!"

"Dad!"

"Mr. Dewey, perhaps you are right," Agent Brand said as he entered the room. "Duncan is an exceptional and brilliant boy, but maybe the life of an agent isn't appropriate for him anymore."

"Alexander!" Ms. Holiday said in complete surprise. "Duncan is one of this country's greatest assets!"

"Find yourself another asset," Avery said. "I'm taking Duncan home. He may wind up below average, but he'll still be alive."

That night, Duncan lay in his room alone. His father had demanded that Duncan hand over the hovering blue orb that gave him access to Benjamin. Without it, he couldn't activate his supercomputer or even access his holographic clothing store. He had no idea what he was going to wear to school the next day.

Worse, no Benjamin also meant no security system in his bedroom. No cameras, no access codes, and no locks on his door. Shortly before ten, his door opened and the Creature crept inside.

"Now you know how it feels," she said.

Duncan stared at her for a moment. "What do you mean?"

"Without your powers you know how it feels to be me," she said. "Average, ordinary, regular. Try being the sister of a superhero. Try being the sister of a genius. Try being the sister of a kid who is so amazing that teachers in *her* classes are already competing to get him as a student."

"You don't have to be average," Duncan said. "You could study. You could get involved in things at school. You could stop being sarcastic and ditch some of the losers you've been hanging out with."

There was a long, silent pause, and then his sister whispered. "So far, it's the only way to get any attention around here."

She turned and closed the door behind her, leaving Duncan alone in the dark. He lay in his bed looking up at the glow-in-the-dark stars his father had glued to his ceiling when they first moved to the neighborhood. That was before he had become a spy or had his imagination inspired by technology. It was when he was just Duncan Dewey, a below-average kid from a below-average school in a below-average neighborhood who had a mother and father who hoped he would be something more. How could he go back to that now?

Duncan did not know when he fell asleep, but he awoke to bright sunshine and someone screaming.

"Benjamin!" he cried as he leaped out of bed. It took him a moment before he realized he no longer had access to his supercomputer. He scowled and threw open his door. Lights were flickering on and off. The television in the living room was changing channels by itself. The vacuum cleaner zipped down the hallway on its own power.

Duncan found his family huddling beneath the kitchen table, under assault by appliances. The freezer door flew open, shooting out ice in all directions. The coffeemaker was spraying steaming hot brew around the room. And the toaster was firing blackened crusts like ninja stars.

"What is going on?" Aiah cried. "Your machines are attacking us!"

"I have no idea," Duncan cried as he swiped the remote off the counter. Unfortunately, no matter how many buttons he pushed, the machines did not stop. "The system is not supposed to let this kind of thing happen. There are fail-safe programs."

The blender fell over and the razor-sharp blades flew out, nearly slicing off Duncan's face.

"We have to get you to safety," Duncan cried, grabbing Tanisha by the hand and pulling her toward the front door. Aiah and Avery followed, dodging a DVD player that spit DVDs with deadly accuracy. The front door opened and shut like the jaws of a hungry tiger.

"What is going on, son?" Avery cried as the family managed to dodge the door and raced out onto the lawn.

Duncan looked up the street. Standing on the corner was Ms. Nesbitt. She had her son's ray gun and was aiming it at their house. He started to march in her direction when the lawn sprinkler system went off and blasted him in the face. The stream was so forceful, he fell backward.

"Ms. Nesbitt, get inside. It's dangerous out here," Aiah shouted to her neighbor. She had no idea it was Ms. Nesbitt causing the chaos.

"If you want to get something done, you have to send a woman," Mama cried. Her face looked wild and angry. "I told Simon you kids would survive."

Just then, there was a loud siren and a booming voice: "Intruder! Intruder!" Then a panel slid away on the roof of their house and a rocket launcher was revealed.

"Where did that come from?" Avery cried.

"It was installed in the middle of the night last January," Duncan explained. "There was some fear that if the truth was ever exposed about me, you would be in jeopardy. It was supposed to keep you safe from an attack. All the other kids have them."

"Get down!" Avery shouted as a rocket roared toward them. The family hit the ground, narrowly missing being skewered by the rogue missile. It crashed into a parked car across the street. The explosion blasted the innocent vehicle into a million pieces and sent choking oily smoke into the winter sky.

"I feel so much safer," the Creature cried.

"Ms. Nesbitt is doing this! We have to get away from her," Duncan shouted.

"What does all of this have to do with our neighbor?" Avery asked.

"Her son is a very, very bad person who created a machine that affects computers," Duncan tried to explain. "It infects them with a virus that makes them susceptible to his commands. Turns out, Ms. Nesbitt is a very, very bad person too."

"Does it work on all machines?" Avery asked.

"No, just ones with processors in them," Duncan answered. "Why?"

"Everyone get to the car," Avery said. "There isn't a silicone chip to be found in Ramona. I built her from the ground up. It's all pistons and gas."

Duncan was stunned. It was a brilliant idea.

The family raced to Avery's Mustang and hopped inside. Avery turned over the engine and soon they were backing out of the driveway just as another missile launched from the roof. It narrowly missed them, allowing the family to tear off down the street.

Duncan spun around in his seat only to see that Mama was hopping into her own car.

"Don't worry," Avery said. "We're safe. Ramona is one hundred percent computer free."

"I'm not worried about our car, Avery. I'm worried about all the others," Aiah cried as a brand new electric car rolled out of its driveway on a collision course with them. Avery swerved in the nick of time, but more cars under Ms. Nesbitt's control rolled onto the road to give chase. Duncan's father slammed his foot on the gas and Ramona took off with a jolt. He handled the car like a seasoned NASCAR driver, turning down alleys and racing past highway entrances and along the river—doing everything he could to keep the family safe.

"I can't believe our neighbor is trying to kill us! Is this because we asked her to trim her hedges?" Avery cried.

"Can't you use any of your goofy spy stuff to help?" the Creature cried.

Duncan shook his head. "Dad took me off the team," he said. "I don't have any of my old abilities." He thought about what he would do with his nanobytes. He'd crawl out of the window, leap from car to car, and snatch the weapon out of that crazy woman's hand. If only he had his nanobytes.

And then Jackson's face flashed in his mind. "Man up, Duncan."

He knew exactly what he had to do.

"Dad, try to hold the car steady," Duncan said as he rolled down the back window.

"Why? What are you going to do?" Avery said.

"It just dawned on me, Dad. I may not fit in with this family, but I'm still a member, and no one messes with the Deweys!" Duncan replied, then squeezed out of the speeding car before his mother could grab his ankle and stop him. The wind was fierce, and even before he got to his feet, he felt as if he might fall. He knew what he was doing was not the action of a sane person, but what other choice did he have? The world was full of technology and Albert's mother could control it until she killed them all. He was just hoping his hands and feet remembered how nimble they could be, sticky or not.

He stood swaying on the trunk of his dad's car, then, taking a deep breath, he leaped onto the hood of the car right behind them. He scampered over the roof and onto the trunk before bracing himself and then taking another leap. On the next car he did the same, only this time his foot sank into the car's soft top. It was a convertible! He pulled his foot free, then slid down onto the trunk, standing again to leap onto the hood of the truck right behind him. Duncan took a bad landing and could feel himself sliding off the front of the truck. He just managed to snatch the grill with his fingers. The metal dug into his skin, hurting more than anything he had ever imagined. What he wouldn't have given for some sticky hands right then! With his feet skidding on the pavement under the truck, he managed to pull himself up and onto the hood again. He scrambled over the cab of the truck and then down into the bed. There he found several potted plants . . . and Ms. Nesbitt's car directly behind him.

Through her windshield he could see her maniacal face. Even Simon didn't have that kind of evil in his eyes. He hefted up a potted plant and tossed it at Ms. Nesbitt's car. It crashed down hard on her hood and exploded with shards of ceramic and clods of soil. She swerved and nearly drove into a ditch before she righted the car. Soon, she returned to her fevered pursuit.

Duncan took another pot and tossed it. This one missed and smashed on the highway. He bent over for another, only to feel the truck screech to a halt. Duncan fell into the bed, slamming into the cab, then ricocheting out the back. He landed right on the hood of Ms. Nesbitt's car.

The two locked eyes, and Ms. Nesbitt threw her car into reverse and gunned the engine. Tires squealed and burned while Duncan snatched the windshield wipers and held on for his life. Mama spun the car around and tore off down the road, accelerating to sixty miles an hour. She turned the wheel one way and then the other, trying to shake off her unwanted passenger.

Duncan reached his hand into the open window, hoping to snatch the ray gun, but Ms. Nesbitt pulled it away.

"You know, you can forget having me mow your lawn anymore, lady!" Duncan shouted.

Frustrated, he pulled the wiper blade off and used it to swat at the woman as she drove. All it did was further aggravate her, and she turned the car into oncoming traffic, all the while firing the ray gun so that cars weaved out of her way.

"You're not going to stop my Albert!" she cried as she gunned her engine once more. The sudden burst of speed was shocking, but Duncan was smart enough to know it meant something

much worse. He turned and saw an auto carrier right in front of him. Ms. Nesbitt intended to ram it, which would certainly mean the end of Duncan Dewey. He braced himself, knowing it was all over, when, suddenly, there was a honk. He looked over and spotted his father's car matching the woman's, speed for speed. Avery edged the car as close as he could and Duncan leaped onto his hood just as the nasty neighbor rammed the truck. An SUV sitting on the upper tier of the auto carrier came loose and rolled back onto Ms. Nesbitt's car, crushing her hood and bringing her car to a halt. She looked stunned but uninjured.

When his father pulled over, Duncan hopped off of the car. "Stay here," he told his family.

Mama had climbed out and was still shaken, but Duncan could see that she was quickly recovering. She leveled the ray gun at a sports car nearby, but before she could send her computer virus, Duncan snatched the weapon from her hand. He eyed it with a grudging admiration. He could see it was a simple design, but the circuitry inside was the true genius. He could have studied it all day, but the woman was already grabbing for it. He knew what he had to do. He tossed it to the ground and stomped on it hard. The ray gun was destroyed.

"This isn't over," she said, shaking a finger at him. Then she ran over to a nearby pickup truck, yanked the driver out of his seat, hopped in, and drove away.

Duncan's family caught up to him as he watched her go.

"Is there anything you want to tell us about the rest of our neighbors?" Avery said.

SUPPLEMENTAL EVIDENCE

The following e-mail was collected and cataloged as evidence in the case against one Heathcliff Hodges, a.k.a. Choppers, a.k.a. Simon. It contains highly sensitive information of a classified nature. Hodges is believed to be the author. The intended recipients were a goon (identity unknown), Albert Nesbitt (a.k.a. Captain Justice), Gertrude Nesbitt (a.k.a. Mama), and two-dozen squirrels.

From: simon@simonsaysobeyme.com
Date: March 29
To: Staff
Subject: **YOUR UTTER INABILITY TO DO ANYTHING RIGHT!!!!!**

Dear staff,

The criminal business is not for everyone. Most people wash out in a couple of months and mysteriously disappear. It's a highly competitive field and stressful, so my approach has always been to keep things light.

Unfortunately, there are those who are taking advantage of my kindness. As they say, familiarity breeds contempt. So I'm immediately requesting that all staff pursue a more professional relationship. In the next couple of days I will be compiling an evil employment handbook that will spell out the following: my expectations for you, a new code of conduct, and info on our new uniforms. The benefits package will be explained, as well as our policy on company holidays and our Secret Santa program.

In the meantime, let's get some things straight. There is no "I" in the word "team," but if you move some letters around you will find that there is a "me." Think of this the next time you wonder, "Who filled my coffee cup with acid?" or "Who just pushed me into the shark tank?" The answer to those questions is me! It's the same answer to the question, "Who is in charge around here?"

If we're going to take over the world, we're going to have to get on the same page, and that includes not taking our one-of-a-kind prototype that hypnotizes machines without permission, let alone allowing it to be destroyed on Interstate 95.

Also, a few of you are spending a little too much time on YouTube. This is a workplace, people.

Thank you for your anticipated cooperation,

Simon

www.simonsaysobeyme.com

15

Albert put on his new work uniform and studied himself in the mirror. The furry costume with its big fluffy tail was humiliating and made it impossible to sit down. But it was nothing compared to the giant buckteeth, attached by a string that wrapped around his mouth. Mama had simply refused and the goon wasn't even asked. How did he wind up being the only one following the new dress code?

He shrugged and studied the new designs for the giant ray gun. With just enough diamonds in their possession, the next step was finding the microchips. To process the information needed for the ray, he would need millions of them. Where was he going to get them?

He had telephoned every microchip manufacturer in the world and no one could sell him nearly enough. Even when you added together the three largest manufacturers—the United States, China, and India—he still could not get a tenth of what he needed. It wasn't a matter of cost. Simon had unlimited resources from all the banks he had robbed, not to mention the countless identities he had swiped using the ray gun on the Internet. There simply weren't enough chips in the world.

The boss would not be happy. His little face would turn bright red and his teeth—oh, those horrible teeth—would glow. Then some horrible cage full of dangerous animals would be rolled out and he would be tossed inside to his doom. Simon had shoved the pizza delivery guy into the komodo dragon tank when he was five minutes late delivering the Crazy Bread.

Still, Albert couldn't help but think his untimely death might be a blessing. He had more than his fair share of doubts about a world controlled by Simon. Mama had negotiated the partnership so that Albert would rule a little less than half of the planet, but most of it was ocean. He had never wanted to rule the world, not even half. All he wanted to do was be a hero. Dying might be a merciful substitute to living in a world he helped destroy.

"What'cha working on, honey?" Mama asked as she climbed up the rope ladder. The goon was behind her carrying a sack of groceries.

Albert shook his head. He didn't trust his mother any more than he trusted the devil. "I was on a Captain America message board arguing about the Super-Soldier serum."

Mama scowled. "Son, when you rule the world you can read all the funny books—"

"Graphic novels!"

"Whatever you call them. You'll have all the time in the world once you're in charge. Until then, you really should be working on our doomsday device."

Albert could see the hope in his mother's eyes and it made him angry. "Sorry to burst your bubble, Mama, but there isn't going to be a doomsday device."

"Oh!" Simon said as he fell out of a branch above and landed on his feet. A half dozen of his furry friends followed. "And why is that?"

Albert gulped but stood his ground. "To operate the machine the way you're hoping, we need processors and microchips."

"They shouldn't be difficult to acquire," Simon said.

"We need millions of microchips," he said.

Simon frowned. He seemed to understand that there would be no way to buy that many.

"We could make more of the smaller models," Albert said, gesturing to a new one he had recently constructed.

"So I can rob banks?" Simon roared. "I am not a bank robber. I'm an evil genius. Evil geniuses take over the world. That's what we do!"

Mama glared at Albert. "Young man, I'm disappointed."

"Listen, maybe we can reconfigure something so it takes over the entire Internet," Albert stammered.

"The Internet? Do you think I can bring the world to its knees by seizing control over a bunch of blogs about *Twilight* and cats playing the piano?" Simon sighed. "Friend, would you show Mr. Nesbitt the extent of my disappointment?"

The goon stepped forward, his hook gleaming in the sun.

"Wait!" Mama cried. "Why can't we just make our own microchips? It might be a pain, but it could be done."

"She's right! Most computer chips are made from silicon," Albert stammered. "But if we made the chips from gallium arsenide and arsenic we would need only a thousand or so. They could conduct the information the ray gun needs."

"I'm aware of arsenic chips," Simon said. "My former teammates have a supercomputer that uses them. They have a staff of scientists who make them."

"So we'll just get some of this gallium stuff and make our own too!" Mama declared.

Simon smiled. "Clever woman, your mother. Albert, where would we get those ingredients?"

Albert looked up at the goon's hook. "I have no idea," he said. "They're both minerals. You'd need to find a huge deposit of them."

"I know where you can get this arsenic stuff," Mama said.

"Albert's father, bless his soul, took me on a vacation to Hawaii. While we were there we went on a tour of the volcano they have on the Big Island. The tour guide said it was a natural arsenic source."

Simon looked skeptical. "And where would we manufacture the chips?"

"That will be easy. I know of several shady factories in New Jersey that can process them with . . . enough pressure exerted in the right place," the goon said.

"See what a great team we are?" Mama said. "Problem solved."

"Should I pack your grass skirt, boss?" the goon asked.

END TRANSMISSION.

YOU ARE BECOMING QUITE THE CODE CRACKER. EVERYONE IS IMPRESSED . . . EXCEPT ME, OF COURSE. I STILL HAVE SOME SERIOUS DOUBTS ABOUT THE THING INSIDE YOUR HEAD YOU CALL A BRAIN, BUT THE PEOPLE IN CHARGE TELL ME YOU HAVE A LOT OF POTENTIAL.

UNTIL I CAN CONVINCE THEM OTHERWISE, I'M FORCED TO KEEP YOUR TRAINING MOVING ALONG. YOU MIGHT ACTUALLY MAKE IT THROUGH MY RIGOROUS TESTS. WE SHOULD PREPARE FOR THAT HIGHLY UNLIKELY EVENT.

THE NEXT CODE IS SO SIMPLE, YOU'LL WONDER HOW ANYONE COULD BE FOOLED BY IT, BUT TRUST ME, KID, LOTS OF PEOPLE HAVE BEEN. IT'S CALLED A TRANSCRIPTION ROUTE CODE, AND EVERY GOOD SPY KNOWS HOW TO DECIPHER IT. FIRST YOU NEED A MESSAGE THAT CONTAINS THIRTY LETTERS, LIKE:

BEANPOLE WAS THE
GREATEST NERD EVER.

(THIS, BY THE WAY, IS NO
SECRET.) NOW, TO PUT IT INTO
A ROUTE CODE, FIRST
TAKE OUT THE SPACES:

BEANPOLEWASTHEGREATESTNERDEVER

THEN ESTABLISH A
ROUTE TO READ IT:

```
S E T A E R
T L O P N G
N E B E A E
E W A S T H
R D E V E R
```

YOU CAN SEE THE "B" NEAR THE
CENTER. READ TO THE RIGHT LIKE
YOU'RE RUNNING A MAZE, THEN UP,
THEN TO THE LEFT, THEN DOWN,
AROUND AND AROUND UNTIL
YOU COME TO THE END.

WHERE THIS GETS TRICKY
IS WHEN YOU USE YOUR KEY
CODE CIPHER CIRCLES. ADDING
THE TWO CODES TOGETHER
MAKES THIS MAD DIFFICULT.
I'VE WRITTEN A SPECIAL
MESSAGE JUST FOR YOU,
PAL. THE KEY LETTER IS
"H"—GOOD LUCK.

```
L M F S S L
L J H D V T
A B P R U Z
A Y L M V Y
Y F Z V H W
```

I FEEL LIKE I'M BEATING
A DEAD HORSE HERE.

LEVEL 6
ACCESS GRANTED

BEGIN TRANSMISSION:

16

38°53 N, 77°05 W

That night, Duncan and his
family camped out on the floor of his Aunt Marcella's home.
Aiah and Avery shared an inflatable mattress. The Creature took
the couch, and Duncan slept uneasily on a reclining chair. He
was fairly certain that without her ray gun, Ms. Nesbitt could
do them no harm, but he had no idea if Albert had built a
second one, or a third, or a dozen. Who knew if he, or Simon,
or the goon was on his way for a second attempt at killing them
all. Much of the night Duncan was awake, keeping a close eye
on the people he loved the most.

His cousin Winston lent Duncan some clothes to wear to
school the next day, but Winston was nearly half a foot taller
than he was. Winston was also a huge fan of hip-hop, so most
of his clothing ran XXL. Duncan took a look at himself in the
mirror and realized he was dressed much like the cool kids at
his school for once. His father lent him his belt to keep his

pants from falling to his ankles, and he headed off to school.

He was certain his new clothes would bring him a lot of unwanted attention. There was nothing worse than a nerd trying to fit in, but much to his surprise few people even noticed. In fact, most of the kids acted as if they didn't recognize him at all. Even Principal Dehaven, who took great joy in abusing him, walked right past him in the hallway.

Flinch did a double take when he sat down next to him in class. "Who are you and what have you done with my best friend?" he asked.

"Listen, I have to see Agent Brand, right away."

"We heard all about the attack," Ruby whispered as she leaned over to join the conversation. "I've ordered agents to watch your family. They've been instructed to steer clear of computer technology."

"I want to talk to Brand. I know my dad yanked me off the team, but I have to do something about Simon and his gang. I can't just sit and watch you guys fight my battles."

Jackson shook his head. "He's busy prepping for our next mission."

"Mission? How come no one told me?" Duncan asked.

"Duncan, you aren't on the team anymore," Matilda replied. "I'm sorry." She smiled sadly at him. "It's not the same without you."

Suddenly, the foursome let out an enormous sneeze. Duncan, however, was fine.

"They turned off my nasal alert?" he cried.

"Just the alarm," Jackson whispered. "Benjamin hasn't gotten around to turning the comlink off yet."

Matilda walked over to the window. "You won't believe this! There's a man outside juggling chainsaws!"

As usual, the entire class leaped to their feet, as did Mr. Pfeiffer.

"Sorry," Flinch said as he ran to the door. A moment later he and the rest of the team had vanished.

This wasn't fair. Duncan had to see Brand right away. He leaped up from his chair and rushed out into the hallway.

"Mr. Dewey! Where do you think you're going?" Mr. Pfeiffer shouted, but Duncan ignored him. He raced down the hallway, where he found Mr. Brand in his janitor disguise mopping the floor.

"Is the mission about Simon?" Duncan demanded.

Brand scowled and ushered the boy into a broom closet, then closed the door tight.

"Have you forgotten that missions and spies are not for the general public's ears?"

Duncan ignored the scolding. "Yesterday Albert's mother attacked my family with the ray gun. We were lucky to survive.

I can't just sit in Mr. Pfeiffer's class while Simon and his gang are running free. You have to let me help!"

Agent Brand looked taken aback by the boy's forcefulness. He eyed him closely but shook his head. Then he went to work moving aside a stack of toilet paper rolls and window cleaner. Behind them was a bright red button mounted on the wall. He pushed it hard and Duncan heard the door lock behind him. A panel on the wall slid open and Benjamin popped out and hovered before Brand's face like a mechanical bumblebee.

"Good afternoon, Agent Brand," Benjamin said. "Former agent Gluestick."

"Just a second, Benjamin," Brand replied, turning his attention back to the boy. "Listen, Duncan. I've read your file. You told the last director you couldn't keep such a big part of your life from your parents. He made the foolish mistake of allowing them to know, and now look where we are. They want you out so you're out. And to be honest, son, I'm not sure you have what I need these days."

"Huh? I'm your best agent!"

"Sure, you are. No arguments. But you're a little lazy."

"What?"

"Duncan, secret agents have lots of gadgets and technology at their disposal, but the good ones don't rely on them. When your upgrades were destroyed, you were practically helpless. You second-guessed yourself and me. I need spies who can get the job done with their brains when all the fancy toys are broken."

The spy unzipped his uniform and stepped out of it, revealing a sharp black tuxedo beneath. He pulled the mop from his bucket and slammed the head on the floor. Duncan watched as it morphed into a white cane. Brand leaned on it as he walked over to the wall and pressed another red button. From the floor, two metal bars rose up. Brand leaned on them.

"But this is personal," Duncan argued.

Brand shook his head. "Son, saving the world is always personal. But for you, it is also over. Go back to class." He grasped the bars, the floor fell, and the entire platform sank at an astonishing rate. A moment later, he was gone.

Duncan rushed out of the closet. "Flinch, can you still hear me?" Duncan called. He muttered to himself, "C'mon. The intercom is still supposed to work!"

"Gaaarrahgghgh!" sounded in his ear. There was a pause and then, "What's up, buddy?"

"I should be going on this mission. You have to help."

There was a long pause. Duncan worried the boy would say no, but then he heard, "Go to the gym and hide behind the bleachers. I'll get you on the ship somehow, but if Brand starts shouting, I had nothing to do with it, cool?"

"Cool. I owe you, Flinch. Oh, find out what's in the mission pack and make one for me." Duncan rushed to the gym, only to see Ms. Holiday locking the double doors at the other end of the room. Sprinting as fast as possible, he raced toward the bleachers, fell to his knees, and slid on the waxed floor until he was safely out of sight. He lay very still, hoping he had not been seen, and when he heard the ceiling retracting he knew it had been his lucky day.

While the School Bus rose up from below, Duncan watched and waited for the secret passage to open. He wasn't disappointed. Soon a team of mechanics in orange and scientists in white rushed through the tunnel and quickly went to work refueling the rocket and running diagnostic tests on its engine and landing gear.

Ms. Holiday directed the work and also double-checked the contents of four black packs that had been wheeled in on a cart. Satisfied, she dropped a homemade cookie into each one, then zipped them up. She then asked an assistant to place them aboard the ship. Agent Brand and the rest of the NERDS entered. Duncan couldn't hear what was going on, but he could see Flinch had an identical pack in his hand. As discreetly as the hyper boy could, he handed the pack to the assistant, who placed it with the others. Duncan made a mental note to buy his friend a case of whoopie pies as a thank-you.

Duncan realized it was time to make his move. He crept

along the wall behind the bleachers, then stepped into a crowd of busy scientists too preoccupied with tests to notice him. He waited patiently, then followed the assistant as he hefted the black packs up the ramp and through the ship's door. When the assistant finished storing the bags and departed, Duncan jumped into the compartment where they had been placed and closed the door tight.

It wasn't long before he could feel the engines rumbling and then the awesome blast as the ship exploded into the sky. He wished he had a more comfortable seat, but he was just happy to be on the mission, even as a stowaway.

He sat in the dark for a long time until the door opened. Luckily, Ms. Holiday didn't even look inside the cabinet as she snatched up the packs and distributed them. Only when she realized there was a fifth pack did she look inside, but Duncan was already slipping it on and racing toward the open door of the rocket.

"Gluestick!" Agent Brand cried angrily.

"Duncan, what are you doing?" Ms. Holiday looked shocked.

Duncan reached into his pack and removed a black helmet. He slid it over his head and flipped up the visor so he could talk. "I'm sorry to disobey you and I know what I'm doing is putting you in a difficult position, but—"

"Duncan, you don't have your upgrades!" Ms. Holiday cried.

"Simon and his gang attacked my family. I can't wait for upgrades," Duncan said. As he leaped out into the sky, he thought he saw a proud smile on Agent's Brand's face.

Duncan had no idea what was below him. As he plummeted through the misty clouds, all he could see was a chain of lush green islands that were getting bigger by the second. He counted eight in all and the largest seemed to be directly below him.

"Hello, everyone," Duncan said.

"Gluestick!" Pufferfish cried. "Where are you?"

"Right above you, I think," Duncan said.

"Does Brand know you're with us?" Jackson asked.

"He does now."

"Excellent!" Braceface laughed. "Glad to have you back."

"Gluestick, I order you to stay where you are!" Pufferfish commanded.

"I'm not sure I can do that," Duncan said. "I'm about a mile above the ground and falling fast."

Pufferfish growled. "You are not a part of this team—"

"Oh, calm down, Pufferfish," Wheezer said. "We wouldn't be NERDS without Gluestick."

"Thanks, guys. Now can anyone fill me in on what we're doing six thousand feet above the Earth?" Duncan asked.

"Hope you like poi, big guy," Flinch's voice said. "We're going to Hawaii."

"What part?"

"The part with the big active volcano," Matilda replied. "Simon stole a hoverplane from a base in California and he's using it to suck something out of the lava. Intelligence has no clue what it could be."

"He's after arsenic," Duncan said.

"To poison people?" Jackson asked.

"No, he's building a bigger version of his machine hypnotizer and he needs lots of superprocessors to make it work," Duncan said. "We use the same kind of chips in Benjamin, only a few of ours equal about ten thousand of what you can buy commercially. To make these chips he needs lots of arsenic, and active volcanoes contain some of the richest arsenic deposits in the world."

"See, Pufferfish! Look what we learn when we bring Sticky with us!" Jackson laughed.

"Well, he better get down here and join us," Pufferfish grumbled. "He's not wearing a Wind Breaker. You think his dad was mad before, wait until he finds out his little boy hit the ground going a thousand miles an hour."

Duncan spotted four black specs against the blue sky—his teammates below. "On my way!" He tilted his body so he was

pointing straight down, and the world suddenly came toward him faster and faster. He was like a human bullet, and in no time was right above his friends. He leveled his body off to allow the wind to slow his descent, then searched for Flinch. The others could have easily helped him get to the ground, but to be on the safe side, he chose his friend with superstrength. Flinch reached out with a free hand and snatched him by the arm. His grip was like a vise.

"Fancy meeting you here," Flinch said.

As they dove, Duncan looked out over the Kilauea crater— the site of one of the world's most active volcanoes. It must have been several miles in diameter with a thick, black crust covering everything. It was awe-inspiring.

"I don't see Simon or a hoverplane," Duncan said.

"He's not down there," Matilda said. "He's a few miles south at a place called Pulama Pali. The flow of lava from the volcano actually travels underground through tubes and comes out on the side of a cliff."

"All right, people," Ruby said. "Let's activate our Wind Breakers."

Flinch's jacket billowed out, slowing their fall. The two boys drifted south with the wind and were soon floating over the rocky Hawaiian cliffs. There, Duncan saw a craft that looked like a combination of a plane and a helicopter. On each side was a huge barrel-like engine that blasted blue flames. A gigantic tube hung from the machine. It was sucking up the horrible ash that covered everything. The arsenic seemed to be sifted through a filter in the back of the ship, and the leftover ash was dumped into the ocean.

Flinch pulled the cord on his jacket, and the tether shot out of the bottom. He and Duncan slid down it to land on a nearby cliff.

"I don't approve of this, Gluestick," Ruby said once everyone had landed. "But if my family were attacked, I'd do the same thing."

"Here's the problem, dude. You're powerless," Jackson said as his braces started to swirl. "We all have the upgrades. We're back online. Are you OK with being a normal kid? No gadgets? No powers?"

Duncan nodded his head. "I'm manning up. Are we going to talk all day, or are we going down into that volcano to kick some bad-guy butt?"

Matilda grinned. "You, my friend, are suddenly the coolest person I know."

The children looked down the cliff face. The lava was flowing in a red, hot stream into the ocean, raising the temperature dramatically and turning the water into thick, muggy steam. It was going to be hot down there. Just above the lava flow, the hoverplane continued its work sucking up minerals off the rocky cliff. Duncan reached into his pack and found some rope, clips, a hammer, and a handful of pins. He pounded a pin into the hard, volcanic rock, then looped the rope around it. Within seconds he was ready to rappel down toward the hoverplane. The others shrugged their shoulders.

"Um, I guess we follow Gluestick," Ruby said.

Matilda snatched Flinch around the waist and then fired her inhalers so the two soared over the edge. Jackson's braces created four long, spindly legs. He took Ruby in his arms and the two crawled over the side.

Duncan struggled with his ropes but refused to ask for help. All of the team had been trained in rappelling, but he remembered not taking it too seriously. He remembered thinking that it was pointless to learn, as he could stick to any surface. If only he hadn't taken the shortcuts. Was Brand right? Was he lazy?

Before he could get too frustrated, he stopped, took a deep breath, and focused on what he had been taught. Ms. Holiday had shown them all what to do. What had she said? *Kick off the side of the cliff and ease the rope through your gloved hand.* He took a deep breath and followed her instructions and it worked. In no time, he was out of rope. He tied himself off and then pounded another pin into the rock and attached a second rope from his pack.

He caught up to the rest of the team yards away from the hoverplane.

"So what's the plan?" Matilda called to Pufferfish.

"I think the best—"

Duncan interrupted Ruby. "Matilda is taking me over there. That's the plan."

Everyone looked at Pufferfish. "Umm."

"No arguments," Duncan said. "This is personal."

Pufferfish nodded.

Matilda took Duncan in her arms and flew him over to the hoverplane. Once there, she used one of her inhalers to blow a hole in the side of the ship. The two spies flew inside the cockpit, ready for a fight . . . but something was wrong. The ship was empty. Glowing letters on the control panel read REMOTE PILOTING ENABLED.

"There's no one here!" Matilda said.

"What?" Ruby said over the nose comlinks.

"Let the lunch lady know we need a pickup. Simon's flying this ship from somewhere else," Duncan said. "He's been playing us since the beginning—running us around in circles, guessing what we'll do before we even do it. He knows us too well."

"No arguments there. But if he's not here, where is he?" Matilda asked.

Duncan had an idea, and the answer made him very, very nervous.

38°53′N, 77°05′E

17

38°53 N, 77°05 W

Albert walked down the halls of Nathan Hale Elementary with a thousand eyes watching his every step. He hadn't been in the school in twenty-five years, not since he had been a student there as well, but that wasn't why the children were watching him. He was wearing his Captain Justice costume and carrying a ray gun. He was also not alone. Simon, with his skull mask and army of hypnotized squirrels, was right behind him. Not to mention the goon with his razor-sharp hook. And Mama—who turned heads with her gaudy jewelry and tiger-print jacket. A rumor began to spread that the foursome were new teachers, which caused many students to faint.

Albert knew they were being gawked at but shrugged it off. Kids had never been kind to him. He remembered how his peers used to break his beakers and contaminate his petri dishes just for fun. He couldn't blame them. Being dressed like a scientist was like taping a sign to him that read PLEASE PUNCH ME AND TAKE MY LUNCH MONEY. Mama had made his life a misery, but soon the bullies and jerks would be begging for his help. Soon he would be the superman he was always meant to be.

"You had to wear the costume?" Simon said to Albert. "You couldn't have put it on after you got your powers?"

"You should talk," Albert said. "Your skull mask doesn't exactly scream sanity."

"Are you calling me a mad scientist? 'Cause I'm an evil genius! There is a big difference," the boy cried.

"Let's just get this over with," Albert said. "We collect the superchips, I get my superpowers, and you shoot the weapon into space and do what it is you plan on doing."

"Boys, this is no time to squabble," Mama said. "We are very close to getting our hearts' desire. Fighting and petty arguing are what always bring the bad guys down. Just keep your eyes on the prize and we'll be fine. You're sure those kids won't swoop in and stop you, right?"

"No worries, Ms. Nesbitt," Simon replied. "They're very busy trying to stop our evil plan in Hawaii. I leaked the information about the volcano to the military when I stole their hoverplane. I knew the NERDS would come running. It's Agent Brand's weakness. He's a preemptive strike kind of guy and thus predictable. Soon, the NERDS will realize they've been fooled again and they'll race back here, but when they arrive, we will have already taken the microchips we need. Unfortunately, we have to wait until they arrive so we can take their rocket. We'll need it to get the machine into space."

"What are you talking about?" Mama cried. "This is just a school. There are no microchips. No rockets!"

Simon stopped at a bank of lockers and opened one of the doors. "Care to fall down the rabbit hole, Ms. Nesbitt?"

Simon stepped in and closed the door.

"He's crazy, right?" Mama said. She opened the door. The locker was empty.

The goon shrugged and crawled in next. Seconds later, he vanished as well. Then it was Mama's turn, and finally Albert's.

He opened the locker door and saw a glowing blue light inside. A calm, female voice said, "Prepare to enter the Playground."

Albert poked his head inside but could not find the source of the invitation. "Hello?"

"Prepare to enter the Playground," the voice repeated.

"How do I do that?"

"Step into the locker for delivery."

Albert eyed the tiny space. "I'm not sure I'll fit."

"Step into the locker for delivery."

Albert crammed a leg into the locker and then squeezed his

massive belly inside. His latex suit made his efforts sound like a clown twisting the world's largest balloon animal. How he managed to get his head inside he would never know, but after twenty minutes of serious effort he finally got the locker door shut behind him.

"I hope this is really the way in, 'cause there is no way I'm ever getting out."

"Delivery in five, four, three, two, one."

The floor beneath Albert slid open, but he did not fall. In fact, he hung above the hole, kicking his feet in hopes of dislodging himself. It didn't work. "I'm stuck!" he cried.

"Administering slippery jelly," the voice said, and a spray of fluid basted him like a Thanksgiving turkey. But he was still crammed in tight.

"Still stuck," Albert said, feeling embarrassed.

"Calculating Plan B. Please hold," the voice said.

"Oh, c'mon!" he cried.

"Prepare for delivery," the voice said as something snatched Albert by the ankle. It felt like a hand and it tugged at him until finally he was dislodged. A moment later he wished he had stayed stuck. His body was thrown through a series of tubes. He rolled through a loopty-loop, then along a conveyor belt, and finally tumbled down a tube and shot out of it like a cannonball onto a hard concrete floor.

He adjusted his mask, which had come askew in the fall, and looked around. His jaw dropped because of what he saw—hundreds of workstations filled with experiments of all kinds, computers with monstrous hard drives, technology beyond anything he had ever imagined. He might have stared at it all day, but then he noticed a tiny blue orb floating about.

"I have alerted security," the orb chirped. "Stay still and you will be arrested at any moment."

"What are you?" Mama asked.

"This is Benjamin," Simon said, making introductions. "Good to see you, old friend."

"Hello, traitor," the ball chirped. "You do not have permission to enter the Playground. Your agent credentials have been revoked. You are a wanted fugitive."

"Hypnotize this thing," Simon cried to Albert. "I've taken care of the others." He gestured to the hundred scientists standing obediently in one corner.

Albert aimed his ray gun at the little blue ball and pulled the trigger. There was a loud screech and the ball smoked as if its circuits were on fire. Then it righted itself.

"How can I help you?" Benjamin asked blandly.

"We're looking to borrow a few of your fancy microchips, Benjamin," Simon said.

"But first, I want my superpowers," Albert said.

"Fine! Benjamin, will you put Mr. Nesbitt through the upgrade process?"

The little ball chirped. "The upgrade process is designed for children. It has never been done on a full-grown adult."

"But that's only because it's programmed not to, right? Not because it can't."

"That's correct."

"Then get started. The rest of us will collect what we need," Simon said, then turned to Albert. "Oh, and allow me to be the first person to say hello to the world's first real superhero."

"Follow me," the orb said. It floated into a tiny room, and Albert tentatively followed. Once inside, a heavy door closed behind him and a chair rose up out of the floor.

"Please have a seat," the ball said.

Albert sat down and was immediately strapped into place. His ray gun fell to the floor. "Hey!"

"Just relax," Benjamin said as a bank of lasers appeared on each wall. Their light beams traced every part of Albert's body. "Scanning for weaknesses. Oh dear. Um, just relax, Albert. This is going to take a while."

DETAILS REGARDING UPGRADE EFFORTS ON SUBJECT ALBERT NESBITT

SUBJECT: ALBERT NESBITT
Weakness Detected—Bad haircut
Weakness Detected—Zero charisma
Weakness Detected—Poor eyesight from endless television watching
Weakness Detected—Permanent stains on lips and teeth from diet consisting entirely of cheese puffs, soda, and delivery pizza
Weakness Detected—Skin cannot handle the sun's radiation due to years of subterranean living
Weakness Detected—Allergies to pollen, peanuts, work, females
Weakness Detected—Poor upper-body strength
Weakness Detected—Oversized thumbs and forefinger muscles developed from video game controller use, also known as Loser Hand
Weakness Detected—Obesity causing tremendous stress on knees, ankles, belts
Weakness Detected—Poor lower-body strength

The flight back to Arlington

was not quiet. Ms. Holiday spent most of it scolding Duncan for disobeying orders and, more seriously, for scaring her half to death. Agent Brand sat nearby, smoldering. He stood up, paced back and forth, then sat down again, only to repeat it all a moment later.

When the School Bus finally landed in the gymnasium, it was met by several panicked scientists.

"There's four of them, not to mention the squirrels," a scientist said between anxious gasps.

"One of them is Choppers and this guy with a hook for a hand. They're tearing up the Playground," another scientist said. "But they're nothing compared to the woman. There's murder in her eyes—pure evil. We snuck out but everyone else is down there with them."

"You didn't mention the other guy with them who was

wearing the goofy costume," the third scientist cried. "I saw them take him into the upgrade room. I think they're trying to give him upgrades."

"There's no need to worry about that," Ms. Holiday said. "Benjamin will only upgrade kids."

"Albert's ray gun could fix that," Duncan said.

Agent Brand's face fell. "Ms. Holiday, suit up. I'm afraid we've been invaded."

Ms. Holiday raced off while Brand took the children through the tunnels that led to the Playground. They found chaos waiting. Tables were turned over, experiments were busted on the floor, and a hundred scientists in lab coats were bound and gagged.

Brand took the gag out of one scientist's mouth. "What's happened?"

"It was Choppers—"

"Where is he?"

"He put that guy in the suit in the upgrade chair and then he and the rest of them emptied out the processors from every computer," the man said.

"All right, you're going to have to be patient. We've got a crisis on our hands and no time to untie you all. It's best if you're out of the way," the agent said. Before he could give more orders, the door to the upgrade room opened and out came Albert Nesbitt.

Duncan was shocked at what he saw. Albert's entire body

was covered in computer ports—for USB cables, FireWire adapters, and all manners of plugs, both foreign and domestic. Albert looked down at himself, perplexed.

"What has happened to me?" he asked. "What kind of superpower is this?"

The Benjamin orb floated around him. It made a series of chirps and then spoke. "Your body is a disaster, Albert. Nearly every physical quality a human being has is a tremendous weakness on you. Your muscles are like those of a kitten. Your skin and teeth are in bad shape. Your bones are truly overworked, and you are entirely too heavy. There isn't enough nanobyte technology in the world for me to make the necessary changes. I was forced to improvise."

"Improvise?" Albert said. "You turned me into a monster!"

"No. On the contrary, I gave you the tools to upgrade yourself. Every single one of the devices implanted in your body allows you to plug in technology and adapt it as your own."

"His upgrade is that he can upgrade?" Matilda said.

Albert still seemed confused. "Show me."

The orb darted across the room and Albert followed, roughly pushing past the team, who stood dumbfounded, not sure what to do. It seemed best to just let Albert discover his abilities so they would have some ideas for how to fight him.

Benjamin stopped at one of the experiment tables, on which

sat a strange-looking pair of glasses. They were enormous, too big for a head, and they had a cable hanging from them that was plugged into a computer. "This is an early prototype for a device that allows the wearer to see through walls."

Duncan knew the glasses. He'd spoken to their creator, Dr. Monroe, many times.

Albert unplugged them from the computer and fastened them into one of his own ports. Suddenly, his eyes glowed a bright green and he looked around the room with wonder. "I can see through everything. I can see the students walking on the floor above this room. Somebody lost a wallet behind this wall. It must have fallen when they were building the school. This is incredible. I have X-ray vision!"

Albert rushed to another table. "What does this thing do?" he asked, grabbing what looked like a piston from an automobile off the table.

"This is a device designed to increase the horsepower of any engine by a thousand."

Albert plugged it in, and again his eyes turned green. In moments he was running around the room at superspeed. "I'm like the Flash!"

"Benjamin, maybe you don't need to help him," Jackson said nervously.

"Oh, your little computer is under my control," Albert said, holding up his ray gun. He waved it in the air and then rushed to another table to snatch up another project and plug it in. "I can turn invisible!"

"Albert, let's slow down a little," Duncan said. "You don't know what a lot of those devices do and you might plug in the wrong thing."

Albert jumped out in front of Duncan. "Look at this," he said as his big hands caught on fire. He waved them around in the air and laughed. The flames did not seem to bother him at all. "I'm a superhero! I'm really a superhero!"

"All right, team," Ruby shouted. "The more gadgets super-crazy plugs into himself, the more unstoppable he becomes. Let's take him down!"

Duncan watched his teammates leap into action. They surrounded Albert and took turns attacking him, but Albert's new powers were already making him a formidable threat. The team was having very little success.

I can't just stand here, Duncan thought. The team needs Gluestick!

Duncan snatched Benjamin out of the air and rushed to the upgrade room. He hoped he had enough time. When the door closed, he pushed a tiny button on the side of the orb and watched all its lights suddenly die. Then there was a hum and the ball chirped.

"Rebooting," Benjamin said.

"Are you back, buddy?" Duncan said.

"Affirmative. That man is not very nice."

"Yes, I agree, and we'll take care of him, but first we have another thing to think about. I need my upgrades, and fast!"

"I'll give you express service, Gluestick!"

The chair rose out of the floor and Duncan hopped into it. His arms and legs were strapped down and the lasers began scanning his body. Duncan closed his eyes, feeling the tiny computers swarming through his bloodstream. He could literally feel them clinging to the sides of his veins, swirling beneath his skin, and shuffling across his bones. He could also hear a tremendous crash outside.

"Just one more moment," Benjamin buzzed.

There was a horrible explosion. It sounded as if the roof had collapsed. Waiting for the upgrade process was excruciating.

"Stop!" Duncan cried as he pulled off the straps. "I can't let them fight him alone."

"But I'm not finished. I can't guarantee your powers are going to work properly."

"I'll have to do it on my own, then!" Duncan shouted. He raced to the door and got a face full of dust when it opened. A huge hole had been blasted in the ceiling, all the way to the sky. Flinch was already leaping upward with Pufferfish in his hands.

Jackson had turned his braces into huge gorilla arms and was hefting himself up as well. Matilda was waiting for Duncan.

"You OK?" she asked. She looked worried.

"Yeah, are you OK?" he asked.

"Sure," she said, grabbing him in her arms. Their faces were closer than ever before. Then she fired her inhalers and they zipped upward, finally landing on the lawn outside the school.

They saw Albert. The man's body had grown to four times its size and he had what looked like dozens of gadgets hooked into his ports, turning him into a walking dynamo of power.

Tiny Pufferfish stood toe-to-toe with the giant. He swung at her, but each time she hurled herself out of the way at just the right time. "Luckily, I'm allergic to getting squashed," she said, scratching at her legs with each life-saving leap.

Albert, however, was becoming enraged. "I have to smash you all so I can go out and save the world!" he bellowed.

"You don't become a superhero doing supervillain deeds, dude," Jackson said as his braces became spikes that poked at Albert's feet. Albert howled in pain, then shot a ball of fire from his hands right at Braceface. The boy's braces twisted and turned into a massive shield that saved him from being broiled. Unfortunately, four more fireballs slammed into the side of the school, setting it on fire. Luckily, it seemed all of the children and staff had been evacuated. Duncan caught a glimpse of them on the other side of the building.

"Hey, loser," Flinch cried as he hopped up and down for Albert's attention.

Albert brought his two fists down hard on the ground, narrowly missing Flinch, who used his superspeed to run between the big man's legs. Now behind Albert, Flinch leaped up and kicked the villain in the rear end. The force of the kick sent Albert flying forward and his head crashed into the cafeteria, breaking the wall and destroying the tables and chairs.

"OK, we can beat up on this guy all day, but what are we going to do to stop him?" Matilda cried. "All those gadgets he plugged into himself are supercharging him with powers. Is there any limit to what he can do?"

And at once, Duncan knew. "Benjamin," he cried, "come with me." And he took off running toward Albert. The gigantic criminal was starting to sit up. He rubbed his head and shook the concrete dust from his torn mask.

"Whatever we're doing," the orb said, "it seems like a very dangerous plan."

"You're the most powerful computer in the world, correct?" he asked as he sprinted onward.

"Correct."

"It must take an awful lot of power to run you," Duncan said.

"It does," the orb replied.

Duncan snatched Benjamin out of the air. "Then let's give Captain Upgrade all the power he can handle!"

By this time, Albert had staggered to his feet. Still dazed, he didn't see Duncan's approach, nor did he see him pull one of the gadgets out of the port on his ankle, remove it from its cable, and plug in the glowing blue ball.

But he felt it.

He let out a howl similar to one you might make if you stuck a fork in a light socket. Beams of bright green energy shot out of his eyes and flew up into the sky. All of the gadgets began to fizz and pop and suddenly blink out, all but Benjamin.

"It's too much power," Albert bellowed. "I can't handle any more!"

"Exactly," Duncan said.

Then, like a tree, Albert fell over and was still.

"What did you do to him?" Matilda cried when she rushed to Duncan's side.

"I crashed his system," Duncan said as he removed Benjamin from the cable. "If he's a walking computer, then there's a way to overwhelm his processors. Too many open applications fried his mainframe."

"*That* problem is solved," Pufferfish said.

"Now we have to stop Simon and Albert's mother," Jackson said.

"But where did they go?" Flinch cried.

Suddenly, they heard a rumbling from inside the school.

"The School Bus!" Flinch shouted.

He led the team back into the school and made a beeline to the gymnasium. Once there, they saw Ms. Holiday in her black spy gear. Brand was nearby in his tuxedo.

"Close the roof!" she shouted, but the rocket was already rising up into the air. Strapped to the side of it was a massive version of the ray gun.

"He's going to activate his machine and there's nothing we can do to stop him," Matilda cried.

"Actually, there is," Duncan said. "But I'll need a ride."

Matilda winked at him and snatched the boy off his feet. Together they rocketed into the air via her inhalers, soaring higher and faster than either had ever gone. In no time they were closing in on the ship.

Duncan looked down at his hands. "I hope there's enough nanobytes in there."

"What are you going to do?"

"Show everyone why I'm on this team," he said, and he

jumped onto the rocket, clinging to the metal skin of the School Bus. Matilda shouted at him.

"Um, when did you get so cool?" she cried, then did something startling. She zoomed up and kissed him on the nose. Then she darted away. Duncan didn't have time to think about the kiss. He wasn't sure how long he could stay attached to the rocket—gravity was pulling at him and the ship was shaking tremendously. He had to get inside fast.

He climbed along the ship's hull until he found the hatch. Then, using every ounce of his strength, he turned the large wheel on the door and watched as the door fell away toward Earth. Moments later he was crawling inside the rocket, much to the surprise of Simon, Mama, the goon, and the squirrels.

"When will you listen to me?" Mama shouted at Simon. "I told you to kill the heroes, but *no!* What would I know?"

Simon shook his head. "So, old friend, here we are again. The world is on the brink of a disaster I created and only you can stop me."

"I'm not your friend, Heathcliff," Duncan said.

"Yes, you're right. It's been a long time since I could call you or any of the team 'friends.' You turned your backs on me, and that's why I have made it my life's work to destroy you. I've studied you all, inside and out, and I know your weaknesses. You, for instance, rely too heavily on gadgets and technology. You could never have guessed they would be your downfall." Simon pulled out another ray gun. He fired it at Duncan, who could feel his nanobytes shutting down. Once again, he was powerless.

"Now you are without your little techy bag of tricks, and I've taken enough superprocessors for my machine. Soon I will have control over every computer in the world and there will be nothing that you or your goofy band of spies can do to stop me."

"So you think you know me, huh?" Duncan said. "You might be surprised. My family doesn't really know me. Agent Brand doesn't even know me. Until very recently, I didn't know myself, but what I've learned is very surprising."

"Oh?" Simon laughed. "I highly doubt that."

"It's not the nanobytes or the gadgets that will help me stop your stupid plan. It's my brain that's going to help me kick your butt." Duncan pulled back and punched Simon in the face. The bucktoothed boy fell backward and slid across the floor. When he got up, his mouth was full of blood and his hands were full of teeth. Two teeth, in fact.

"What have you done?" Simon lisped. His mouth had a huge

hole where his big choppers used to be. "You've . . . you've—"

"My brain told me a good pop in the mouth would stop you," Duncan said. "Pretty smart, huh?"

Simon turned to his squirrels. "Go get him, you good-for-nothing freeloaders."

The squirrels stood still, shaking their heads back and forth and looking utterly confused.

"Didn't you hear me? I commanded you to—" Then Duncan saw a flash of understanding in the villain's eyes. The squirrels had been under his command for a long time. They weren't his partners. They were his hostages. And now they were suddenly free and they wanted revenge.

Simon's furry minions turned on him, and months' worth of rage came out as they scratched at him and hurled nuts in his face. He fell to the ground, unable to defend himself.

"So that's how you take over the world, kid?" Mama shouted at Simon.

"Two down, two to go," Duncan said. "I just fried Albert's brain. He won't be causing any more problems."

Mama snarled. "I'm taking over this operation. I'm going to show you all how it's done, and the first thing we're going to do is kill the hero. Do it!" she shouted at the goon.

The goon looked at Mama and shrugged. Then he flashed

his hook at Duncan. Its silver edges glimmered almost as much as his wicked smile. Then he lashed out at the boy.

Duncan leaped out of the way just in time. He stumbled over a chair. The goon slashed at him again, opening the leather seat of the chair and sending stuffing flying.

"C'mon kid," the goon said as Duncan stumbled toward the back of the rocket. "There's no escape."

Duncan was backed up against a bank of computer monitors. The goon was mere inches away. He raised his hook high in the air and brought it down hard and fast. Duncan ducked and heard a crash. Sparks showered down on him, and when he looked up, he realized the goon was shaking uncontrollably. His metal hook was impaled in one of the TVs, and electricity was coursing through him.

Duncan flipped off the power and the man tumbled to the ground, unconscious.

"Enough!" Mama screamed. "I'll do it myself!" With rage in her eyes she lunged forward and grabbed Duncan by the shirt and threw him toward the open door of the rocket. Duncan grabbed on to Mama to save himself and they both went tumbling out of the ship into the open sky. They turned end over end as the hungry earth below pulled them ever closer.

But then Matilda was there, with an arm around Duncan's

chest, stopping his fall. Duncan tried to hold on to Mama, but the old woman squirmed like a cornered animal and pulled herself from his grip. All Duncan and Matilda could do was watch as Mama disappeared into the clouds.

38°53 N, 77°05 W

38°53 N, 77°05 W

Agent Brand was sorting through the remains of the Playground. Everywhere he looked was destruction. More than forty years of history was completely destroyed—all of it under his watch. It was all he needed to make his decision. He stepped over to the glass table and used his sleeve to wipe off a thick layer of black dust. Then he activated the communications system. One lone computer monitor lowered from above. It blinked to life, revealing a grizzled general with a head shaped like a bullet.

"I'm sorry to bother you, General Savage, but I have something important to discuss about the team."

General Savage cocked a curious eyebrow. "I always have time for you, Brand."

"I have concerns about the future of this—" Suddenly, the screen went black.

"General? General?"

Ms. Holiday stepped out from behind a column. She was holding a black cord—one that was supposed to be plugged into the wall. "We're having technical difficulties."

"Ms. Holiday—"

"Sit down, Alexander. I have something to say to you," the woman replied.

Agent Brand shook his head but did as he was told. He was too tired to argue.

"So you want to shut the team down?" the librarian continued.

Agent Brand nodded. "Look around you. This is not the result of a team that can handle big problems."

Ms. Holiday looked around. "I disagree. I think this is all the evidence you need to prove that these kids can be counted on to save the world. If they hadn't done what they did, the whole planet would look like this."

"They're children," Brand said. "I can't trust their judgment."

"This isn't about their judgment, Alexander. It's about yours. Heathcliff betrayed you and you feel like you should have seen it coming. You're mad that a little boy deceived you and you're using your bruised ego as an excuse to get out of this job."

Brand raised his eyebrows in surprise. It was like Holiday was reading his mind. He realized then that this woman, this beautiful, talented, amazing spy could also be his friend.

"Well, snap out of it, you crybaby!" Ms. Holiday said.

Brand nearly fell out of his seat.

The librarian continued. "You agreed to take on these kids. You agreed to lead them and help them to make the world safe. So one of them betrayed you! Are you telling me you've never worked with a double agent or someone who went rogue? Was Heathcliff Hodges the first person to surprise you? If so, you have been the most sheltered secret agent in the world, buddy. Now stop feeling sorry for yourself. You've got to reinstate Duncan and get the Playground back in working order, and—"

"Is this a man-up speech?" the spy asked.

Ms. Holiday couldn't help but smile. "Yes, it is."

The handsome agent sat quietly for a long moment. "Your message is received loud and clear, Ms. Holiday."

"Good!" the woman cried, though she seemed surprised that he didn't put up a fight. "Now let's stop all the pity parties and get to work. We've got a world to keep an eye on."

Brand grinned and Ms. Holiday stared. "I've never seen you smile. You should do more of it."

Brand frowned but then laughed.

Then Ms. Holiday handed him a slip of paper.

"What's this?"

"It's a secret code, Alexander. The next time you need to talk to someone, use it."

Brand looked down at the slip of paper. It was Ms. Holiday's phone number.

"You could also use it to explain why you were jealous of Captain Blancard," she continued.

Brand was going to argue, but Ms. Holiday stopped him.

"Just call me," the beautiful librarian said. "I don't want to have to give you another man-up speech."

"Allen wrench," Avery said.

Duncan found it in the toolbox and handed it to his father, who was lying under the Mustang. His father's oil-covered hand snatched it and disappeared.

"Thanks, son."

"So, what are you doing under there?"

Avery rolled out from under the chassis. He was lying on a wooden dolly. "Why don't you come down and take a look for yourself?"

Duncan put down the tools and eased himself onto the dolly. When he was comfortable, his father rolled them both underneath the car. Duncan marveled at the many parts of the Mustang. With the help of a handheld light, he could see hoses, tubes, and belts. There must have been hundreds of different mechanisms that made the car go. Not one of them was computerized.

"I'm changing the oil," his father said. "And taking a look at the breaks. They felt a little spongy after our run-in with Ms. Nesbitt. I want to be prepared the next time one of our neighbors tries to kill us."

"Dad, you work on cars all day. I could have the scientists from the Playground come out here and do this for you," Duncan said.

Avery nodded. "I like knowing I can do a few things for myself."

"Without technology." Duncan sighed.

"It's not that I'm against computers and gadgets, Duncan," Avery said. "But as you get older you'll find those things often fail you. If the power goes down, you lose all of them, and then it's just you and a candle while you wait for someone smart, like those scientists, to come and fix it. I like knowing I can fix things myself. I like the connection my brain has to my hands."

Duncan lay there close to his father and realized that they weren't all that different.

"So, can you teach me how the car works?"

Avery laughed. "Not in one afternoon, son, but I'd be happy to tell you what I know."

Suddenly, they heard footsteps and the Creature's voice. "I'm going to kill him!"

Avery and Duncan shared a knowing look, then slid out from under the car.

"Kill who, Tanisha?" their father asked.

"TJ," she cried. "He's cheating on me."

"Who is TJ?" Avery asked.

Suddenly, Benjamin floated into the garage. "Her boyfriend. She's been using me to spy on him all afternoon, accessing satellite imagery. She wanted to fire a drone missile at his house, but I wouldn't let her."

"Tanisha!" Duncan cried. "Those satellites belong to the United States government."

"Honey, when Duncan agreed to let you use his computer, he didn't mean you could use it to invade other people's privacy."

"Then I guess you're probably not going to be happy that I turned TJ in to the NSA as a suspected terrorist. All right, fine. I'll fix it. It's just—well, to be honest, I'm sort of starting to dig the computer. I seem to have a connection with it. I guess it runs in the family."

Duncan smiled.

Aiah came out to the garage. "Well, word is that the school is a disaster. They're shutting it down until they can repair the damage that wacko did to it."

"The team is going to be operating out of a few empty offices at the Pentagon for the time being," Duncan said.

"So Dad changed his mind about you being a spy?" Tanisha asked.

Avery shrugged. "The world needs him."

"Yeah, I talked to Agent Brand myself and he suggested I could get upgrades, too," Tanisha replied.

"Stick to abusing your boyfriend's civil rights," Aiah said. "This family can handle only one spy at a time."

"So what are they going to do about school?" Avery asked his son.

"I guess they'll have us take classes in trailers for now. Agent Brand, Ms. Holiday, and the lunch lady are already setting up access to the Playground."

Suddenly, Duncan let out a powerful sneeze.

"Uh-oh!" Aiah cried. "Please tell me that was hay fever."

"Sorry, duty calls," Duncan said.

"Son, I can't drive you," Avery said. "The car is a mess."

Duncan leaped up and snatched a backpack out of the car. He strapped it to his back and two metal handles popped out. He squeezed them and a rocket lifted him off the ground. "No need, Dad. The GV-761 Rocket Backpack will get me there."

"I thought you had learned a lesson about doing things without fancy technology!" Avery cried.

"I did, Dad, but isn't this the coolest thing ever? I can go from zero to a hundred miles an hour in two seconds!"

Duncan saw his family's disappointed expressions.

"Fine! I promise to take the bus home," he said with a grin. Then he rocketed away, leaving the Dewey family looking at the clouds.

THE END.

ALL RIGHT, ALL RIGHT.
YOU DID IT.
CONGRATULATIONS.
YOU CRACKED THE CODES.
I'D LIKE TO THINK I HAD
A LITTLE SOMETHING TO DO
WITH YOUR SUCCESS. I MEAN,
I ALWAYS KNEW YOU
HAD IT IN YOU.

WHAT?

WELL, I DIDN'T EXACTLY
CALL YOU A LOSER. YES,
I MAY HAVE SUGGESTED
THAT YOU WOULD FAIL.
BUT IT WAS ALL IN
GOOD FUN. YOU KNOW,
I WAS TRYING TO SPARK
A DESIRE TO PROVE
ME WRONG. YEAH.
THAT'S WHAT I WAS
DOING . . .
AND IT WORKED!

ALL THOSE PUT-DOWNS AND INSULTS MADE YOU INTO A FIRST-RATE SECRET AGENT. WHEN THE PRESIDENT AWARDS YOU THE MEDAL OF FREEDOM SOMEDAY, I CERTAINLY HOPE YOU THANK ME, THE GUY WHO MADE IT ALL POSSIBLE. I MEAN, IF I HADN'T SEEN YOUR POTENTIAL WHEN EVERYONE ELSE WAS READY TO GIVE UP ON YOU, WELL, WHO KNOWS WHERE YOU WOULD HAVE ENDED UP!

YOU'RE NOT BUYING ANY
OF THIS, ARE YOU?

FINE . . . FINE.

SO, YOU ARE NOW
OFFICIALLY A MEMBER
OF NERDS, WITH ALL
THE PRIVILEGES AND
RESPONSIBILITIES. I'D
LIKE TO WELCOME YOU
PERSONALLY, BUT YOU'LL
HAVE TO CRACK ONE
MORE CODE BEFORE
WE CAN MEET.

HERE'S YOUR LAST
SECRET CODE.

GO TO

WWW.TEAMNERDS.COM/QRCODE

FOR MORE INSTRUCTIONS.

I'LL BE WAITING.

AND HEY, WASH THOSE
FEET, 'KAY?

END TRANSMISSION.

Acknowledgments

Many secret agents to thank: Susan Van Metre for believing in this series; Chad W. Beckerman for his inspired art direction and Ethen Beavers for his fantastic art (you are why kids buy these books!); Jason Wells, who shouts to the heavens about what I do; as well as everyone at Amulet Books for their incredible support.

Thanks to Alison Fargis and her entire team at the Stonesong Press. Thanks to Alison for marrying me, and giving me Finn, too. Thanks to Joe Deasy for being an eager reader, even after a dozen drafts. Thanks to Howard Sanders and his lovely family: Zoe, Sylvie, and Phoebe. Thanks to Lauren Meltzner, and everyone at UTA. Thanks, thanks, thanks!

About the Author

Michael Buckley, a former member of NERDS, now spends his time writing. In addition to the top-secret file you are holding, Michael has written the *New York Times* bestselling Sisters Grimm series, which has been published in more than twenty languages. He has also created shows for Discovery Channel, Cartoon Network, Warner Bros., TLC, and Nickelodeon. He lives with his wife and their son, but if he told you where, he'd have to kill you.

This book was art directed and designed by Agent Chad W. Beckerman. The illustrations were created by Agent Ethen Beavers. The text is set in 12-point Adobe Garamond, a typeface based on those created in the sixteenth century by Claude Garamond. Garamond modeled his typefaces on ones created by Venetian printers at the end of the fifteenth century. The modern version used in this book was designed by Robert Slimbach, who studied Garamond's historic typefaces at the Plantin-Moretus Museum in Antwerp, Belgium.